Rave Reviews for Gerri Russell

SEDUCING THE KNIGHT

"Action and wildly exhilarating adventure propel the second book of the Brotherhood of the Scottish Templars series forward. Russell packs the pages of the Indiana-Jones-meets-Lara-Croft tale with nonstop action."
— RT BOOKReviews

"This is the second in the Brotherhood of the Scottish Templars series and Russell has her work cut out for her. I love the change of scene to the lands around the Mediterranean and the introduction of the paranormal. This creates a whole new aspect and brings out the power of the biblical elements. A good story for Russell fans."
— Fresh Fiction Reviews

"Russell transports our hero and heroine across vivid locales spanning Spain, the Holy Land, and Scotland – as only an adventure of these epic proportions deserves. The combination of such vibrant descriptions of the environs, a fast-paced storyline, and the quintessential quest for the Ark of the Covenant makes for a very quick and pleasant read."
— Romance Junkies

"This highly charged romance portrays the emotional agony of a stalwart hero and the woman who comes to love him. Medieval enthusiasts will thrill to this adventurous love story and its explosive conclusion."

— RT BOOKReviews

"[*To Tempt a Knight*] has all the elements: a powerful and handsome hero, a vulnerable but determined heroine and a long journey that forces them together intimately. Romance and treasure make a combination that's hard to beat and Russell fans will not be disappointed."

— Fresh Fiction

"*To Tempt a Knight* is a thrilling, fast-paced romance jam-packed with adventure…. Russell cleverly melds historical romance with religious history, with the crux of the story steeped in the noble effort to find the Spear of Destiny and keep it safe from would-be tyrants. To Tempt a Knight is a well-researched history lesson made into entertainment. Intense action sequences ensure the action plays out like a film in the mind's eye of the reader, while complicated, dramatic emotions tug at the reader's heart strings."

— Romance Junkies

I0539785

"Gerri Russell's creative imagination enthralls me. I was hooked from the very first page."

— New York Times Bestselling Author
Debbie Macomber

"The passion and vibrant excitement of the Middle Ages glows on every page of Russell's latest thrilling, emotionally captivating romance, book three in her Stones of Destiny trilogy."

— RT BOOKreviews

"*Warrior's Lady* is heart-melting passion, a powerful story of hate turning to love and being able to trust again. This tale brought a tear to my eye and a pang to my heart as I flipped the pages. Warrior's Lady is definitely a book that historical readers will love."

— Fresh Fiction

"Gerri Russell is an author for the Medieval lover who cherishes both history and the mythical, magical medieval world."

— Merrimon Reviews

"*Warrior's Bride* is a poignant, powerful read. Don't miss it!"
— New York Times Bestselling Author Sabrina Jefferies

"A captivating, heartfelt love story born of strength, survival and et ernal trust. Ms. Russell gifts us with a remarkable story that touches the heart. The ending is nothing short of exhilarating... You don't want to miss this one!"

— Fresh Fiction

"Russell, winner of the American Title II contest, returns with her second powerful medieval romance touched with magic and passion. This well-paced, emotional, poignant drama enhances the romance just as the paranormal elements merge perfectly in Russell's capable hands."

— RT BOOKReviews

"Ms. Russell has created two strong characters able to rise above all that fate and nasty fathers can throw at them... But the journey to the breathtaking conclusion gets more and more intriguing. The primary relationship... takes center stage with the suspenseful plot, but the other characters and the question of loyalty and redemption of past deeds adds to the richness of the whole."

— Romance Reviews Today

"Russell debuts with an action-packed, emotion-driven story that immediately captures your attention. Readers yearning for strong heroines and masterful men will find them here, along with a carefully plotted story. Russell's fresh voice secures her a place on the to-buy list."

— RT BOOKReviews

"*The Warrior Trainer* is a romantic, action-packed story. Scotia is as hard as stone, except when it comes to those she loves. The characters are lovely and the story line will keep you coming back for more. I highly recommend this debut novel from talented new author Gerri Russell."

— Fresh Fiction

"*The Warrior Trainer* is an intelligent, heart-wrenching historical romance that convincingly and seamlessly weaves actual history and mythical fiction together in a work of literary craftsmanship. Gerri Russell has succeeded in rendering emotions, both ecstatic and agonizing, onto the written page. Pangs of joy and grief will linger long after the read is done. *The Warrior Trainer* is a wonderful gift from a very talented author."

— Romance Junkies

Gerri Russell
Border Lord's Bride

My deepest thanks to Andrea Heuston, Steve Ahlbom, Kate Race, Rian Fiske, Carrie Meredith and Dawn Jones of Visual Quill. You gave my dreams a push with your creative energy and helped them fly once more. For that I am forever grateful.

ISBN: 978-0-9838-9979-2

Chapter One

A bitter chill having little to do with the winter weather ripped through Lucius Carr's soul. He reined his horse to a stop atop the hill just above his home. The manor house of the earls of Carrick sat at the bottom of the hill, flanked at each side by a tangle of rosebushes long since gone to their winter slumber. Yet in the summer their splendor would once again erupt into the joyous jumble his mother had so loved. Her home. Her flowers. Her children. She had nurtured them all.

'Twas probably a blessing then that she no longer lived to see what had become of her beloved family. Her sons had suffered terribly, and her girls might yet, if Lucius didn't keep heading toward the manor and accept the earldom.

Except that he didn't deserve the earldom, or any joy that might come from it all. His brother Marcus's words on the day he'd left Midwick Manor came back to him the way they always did in the darkness of the night. You're running away from your family, your responsibility, and yourself, Lucius. You need to stay and fight for what it is you want in this life. If you don't, then you don't deserve anything good to come your way.

He had run that day, away from Marcus, away from his responsibility, as far and as fast as he could toward a dark and dangerous road with the Scottish Templars. But he hadn't traveled alone. His younger brother Peter had insisted on joining him. A familiar twist of guilt centered in Lucius's gut. Peter had followed him and had been burned at the stake by a madman as a result. All the Carr men had died, leaving only him.

A stinging regret mixed with a deep sense of grief, for all he'd run away from. His father had died weeks after his own departure. Marcus was dead these last two months, after a border raid by the English. And that wasn't all he'd lost.

His gaze drifted to another manor house in the distance, nestled in the woodlands as though content to disappear into the trees. At times he'd wished it had, along with those who resided there. His temper flared for a heartbeat before he squashed the sensation. He would no longer be molded by her whims. Nay, Elizabeth Huntingdon had no place in his life. She might be his neighbor, but that was all she'd ever be to him.

The only people who had any importance in his life were his sisters. They were the reason he was here, the reason he'd stopped running. Ruthlessly he shoved away his sense of loss and spurred his horse into a gallop, skimming the grassy field separating him from his home.

As dusk fell over the land, light spilled from three pairs of tall, narrow, leaded windows on the upper levels of Midwick Manor. The windows below were shuttered tightly against the cold of the late afternoon. Smoke from two chimneys wafted up toward skies that appeared ready to open any moment and release their burden of snow.

He made his way across the bridge dividing the manor house from the loch on the eastern side of their…his property. As his horse's hooves clipped across the wooden slats, Lucius's irritation sparked yet again. No one— neither a guard nor a retainer—challenged his approach.

Lucius didn't sense danger, but that didn't mean it wasn't there. He gripped his still-sheathed sword's hilt with white-knuckled force. He'd returned to what remained of his family. He'd promised to spare them from penury and keep them safe. He would educate them to the dangers lurking in the shadows, set a guard, and build up Midwick Manor's defenses. And with luck, it would be enough.

When he reached the stables, he startled the youth sweeping the floor. "Might I help ye, sir?" The lad's eyes widened as Lucius swung down from his horse. He bowed deeply and dropped his gaze to his feet. "Forgive me, milord! I dinna recognize ye."

"Give my horse a good rubdown and a bucket of oats." Lucius softened his tone as he handed the reins to the lad, then slipped a coin into his hand at the same time. "I've been gone a while, that much is true. But I'm back to stay."

The lad's eyes fixed on the coin. "Welcome home, milord."

"Where are the guards?"

" 'Tis only me, milord."

Lucius's hand tightened on his sword. He made his way down the finely laid brick pathway winding toward the massive oak doors that would take him inside. He hardly noticed the heavy wooden arches that made up the ceiling of the entryway and paid no attention to the walls of the hallway lined with the portraits of past earls of Carrick. He strode silently toward the back of the house with one purpose only, to find his sisters. The sound of laughter came from the room his mother had termed the ladies' parlor.

He came to an abrupt halt at the entrance to the chamber and relaxed his grip on his weapon, taking in the sight of his five sisters. They were not little girls anymore, but pretty young women. Lucius studied their animated faces and let their chatter flow over him. Something raw sliced him inside, revealing wounds that had never healed during his absence these last five years. He clenched his hands, then flexed them, wishing desperately he could capture this moment on canvas, stop time and guilt and pain, by indulging himself in a way he'd abandoned since he'd left.

He wished now that he had taken the time to paint Peter and Marcus, even his father, before they died. But that wasn't to be. Lucius drew a sharp breath. Suddenly all eyes turned toward the door.

As the room erupted in squeals of delight, his pain and regrets faded. A heartbeat later he found himself enfolded in his sisters' embraces—all five of them at once. He pressed his cheek to Rose's head and drew in a breath of her sweet scent. Flowers. He'd forgotten they perfumed themselves to smell like the flowers they were named for. Rose, Camellia, Heather, Iris, and Lily.

"Lucius! You're home! We've missed you! You look different. Welcome back!" They were all talking at once and laughing.

And the memory of what he'd run away from flooded him. His throat went tight and his chest ached at the warmth of his sisters' love. He swallowed roughly as he tried to force the unfamiliar sensations away. It was too much. Much more than he deserved. He deserved only darkness and shadows and pain for what he'd put them through.

He wasn't sure when the girls' laughter changed to tears, but it did.

"We've been without a brother for two months now," Camellia cried.

"We didn't know what was to become of us," Rose whispered as the girls clung to him. "We would have lost everything if you hadn't come home."

Lucius simply held them in return and tried to fight a deep sense of guilt as tears burned the back of his own throat. "We are together now," he said over the girls' blonde heads. "Nothing and no one can tear us apart."

It seemed like forever until the weeping turned to sniffles and soft hitches of breath. Slowly, the girls peeled themselves away. Rose, the eldest, separated herself first. She stepped back toward the hearth and delicately swiped at the tears still lingering on her cheeks with the back of her hand.

Rose had matured into a beautiful young lady. He frowned at the realization that she must be close to eighteen now. Instead of socializing with other boys and girls her age, she'd been forced to take up much of the responsibility he had forsaken. Lucius offered her as brotherly a smile as he could muster. He'd make it up to her. Somehow he'd see that she reclaimed that part of her youth he'd denied her.

"Would you like some tea, brother?" Camellia asked as she, too, pulled out of his grasp. She twisted her long golden hair over her shoulder as she turned her attention to pouring out a cup of steaming beverage. Lucius did not miss how the cup trembled in her hands as she did. Camellia was the beauty of the family. At sixteen, she too deserved to be far more social than her current situation allowed.

Heather hiccupped loudly and ruffled her hand through her short, pale gold curls as she detached herself. "You cannot know how worried we were after Marcus died. Uncle Horatio kept coming to visit, and every time he came, more of the servants disappeared. We have only Hadwell and Marie to care for us now."

Heather sank into a chair next to a table holding several stitchery looms and a mass of tangled thread. The fourteen-year-old picked up one of the looms, bowed her head, and fixed her attention to the embroidery she'd abandoned upon his entrance. But even her sudden feigned absorption didn't hide the fear etched plainly on her thin face.

"Only Hadwell and Marie remain?" Lucius asked, dropping his gaze to the two sisters still in his arms. They'd had two score servants, at one time.

"Heather is exaggerating," Camellia said in her clear,

melodic voice. "There are others, but not many."

Iris clung to his leg as though refusing to let go of him ever again. She had grown so much since he'd seen her last. She must be nearly eight years old now.

Lily had been an infant when he'd left. The youngest, at six, she pulled away from his other leg and nodded, sending her golden curls bobbing.

Lucius frowned. There had to be more to the story, something the girls weren't saying. "I'm here and willing to take my place as your guardian and as the Earl of Carrick. Uncle Horatio has no further claim to Midwick Manor now that I am home."

"Not unless you die," Iris said with a slight lisp, her lips turned down in a pout. She gripped his leg all the harder.

"Well, it's settled then, because I have no intention of dying." He gave Iris a squeeze and disentangled her from his leg with a cheerful smile, despite the sudden unease his sisters' words had sparked in him.

The room erupted into conversation once more as his sisters hurled one question after another at him.

"What was it like being a Templar?" Rose asked, edging closer to him, her face alight with interest.

"Did you have to kill anyone?" Iris asked with a frown.

"Were you lonely without us?" Camellia plopped into the chair opposite Heather and plucked at the embroidery threads on the table between them.

"Heaven above, what's with the chatter?" a familiar voice called from the hallway. Hadwell hastened through the doorway, his gaze passing over each sister until it came to rest on Lucius. The estate's steward startled for a moment before his face wreathed in a smile. "Praise the saints! Lord Carrick. From the message ye sent, we weren't expectin' ye to arrive 'til tomorrow. Marie'll be in a tither when she finds out. She was savin' the hindquarter for supper tomorrow." The middle-aged man, who'd spent forty of his fifty years in service at Midwick Manor, expelled a soft grunt as he bowed.

Lucius placed a hand on the retainer's shoulder, encouraging the man to rise. "We need not be so formal, Hadwell."

"Me old back thanks ye, lad." His eyes went wide. "Forgive me—milord."

Lucius turned back to the room. "Girls, excuse me. We can talk more over supper. Hadwell and I have things to discuss." Lucius turned to his steward. "Come," he said, setting off for the great hall, where they could talk more openly. He paused before the arched oak double doors. "I need to know everything that has happened here at Midwick Manor since I've been gone." He pushed the doors open and signaled Hadwell to enter.

The man hesitated, and wariness flickered in his eyes for an instant before the look vanished. He stepped inside the empty hall. "Ye and Peter, God rest his soul, have been gone, what, five years, followin' the Templars?"

Lucius flinched at the mention of Peter's name, then nodded impatiently. He moved toward the hearth and the two long benches angled in front of the open grate. "Tell me, Hadwell. What is happening? Why is my father's brother scaring off the staff?"

Hadwell slipped onto the bench as though his legs were

no longer able to support him. "While yer father yet lived all was well. 'Tis only when Marcus inherited that things turned rough."

Lucius sat on the bench near the fire. Warmth enveloped him, yet did nothing to relieve the chill that had settled inside. "Rough. In what way?"

"Yer brother did well enough, and the estate produces well, at least it did. The troubles started after Marcus died. That's when most of the servants and some of the crofters disappeared after yer uncle's visits. Lucky fer us 'tis winter and the crops are yet tae be sowed."

Lucius stood and paced before the fire. "What could Horatio possibly gain by crippling the estate? And why are the servants leaving? Many of them have spent their entire lives here at Midwick."

" 'Tis troubling," Hadwell agreed as he stood also. "He must be offerin' them somethin' they can't say nay tae."

Lucius stopped in front of the faithful steward. "Thank you for staying with the girls, Hadwell. Your loyalty will not go unrewarded."

The old man grinned. " 'Tis and has always been a pleasure tae serve yer family."

The tension in Lucius's shoulders eased. "I'll be needing you now more than ever to guide me. I've been a warrior for so long, I've forgotten all else. I'm ready to assume my responsibilities."

Hadwell's gaze fixed on his face. "All of 'em, milord?"

"Of course." He frowned suspiciously. "Why?"

" 'Cuz there's one obligation I'm nae sure ye'll like. There's nay way out of it though. 'Tis almost as if the previous Lord Carrick knew—"

"Hadwell. Speak plainly."

"Yer tae be married in four days, milord."

Chapter Two

Lucius shook his head dazedly. "Married? To whom?"

Hadwell worried his hands as he took a step back. "Tae Elizabeth Huntingdon."

Elizabeth. Lucius felt as though someone had hit him in the gut with a mailed fist and knocked the breath out of him. He stilled. "You cannot be serious."

"Deadly serious, I'm afraid." The old man pursed his lips and rocked back on his heels. "The terms were quite clear. When ye accepted the title as the Earl of Carrick, ye accepted all that went with it, including the betrothal of Miss Huntingdon tae the Earl of Carrick. That's ye."

Lucius shifted his gaze to the flames in the hearth. The news about his uncle's visits and disappearing servants and crofters was unsettling enough. And he was expected to marry on top of that? "I would rather burn as Peter did than wed that woman."

"If ye don't go through with it we'll all suffer. The marriage was tae bring the two properties together tae help strengthen our defenses against the English. That's yer fight now."

Lucius jerked his attention back to his steward. "I'm done with fighting."

Hadwell shook his head. "The English raidin' parties have started again. None of us are safe."

Lucius stared at the man, hard. He could feel a tic in his jaw leap along with the pounding of his heart. It took everything he had to keep himself in check. He could fight the English. He could help protect his country, but he could not, would not, marry Elizabeth.

Hadwell's features softened. "I know this is nae easy fer ye. I remember how 'twas between the two of ye. The marriage will nae bring any funds tae the estate, quite the opposite in fact. But think of yer sisters. They need a woman's influence as they enter their own marriageable years. Ye need a woman's touch around here. Especially with the servants gone, there's much tae be done. Think on it, milord. 'Tis fer the best, ye'll see."

"Does Elizabeth know?" Lucius asked.

"Aye." Hadwell's face turned pink.

"Has she anything to say about this arrangement?"

"There's nothing she can say, milord. She needs this marriage as much as ye. 'Tis done," Hadwell said dully.

Nay, what had sparked between Elizabeth and him five years ago was certainly not done. But it would be soon if he had anything to say in the matter.

He'd accept the earldom, but not the woman who came along with it. She'd rejected him once. She wouldn't get the chance to do it again.

❧

Elizabeth Huntingdon strode slowly away from Huntingdon Hall until she came to the slight rise in the land dividing her father's property from that of Midwick Manor. Standing in the semidarkness, she pulled her woolen shawl more tightly around her shoulders against the falling snow. Through a veil of white she trained her gaze on the dark figure on a dark horse in the distance.

Lucius Carr had come home.

She wasn't expecting him until tomorrow, yet somehow she knew… Her steps had led outside before she knew where she was headed. A harsh breath escaped her. She tipped her face up to the night sky. Snow caressed her cheeks but did nothing to soothe the turmoil that twisted inside her. She closed her eyes, praying Lucius would not hate her all the more for the agreement that had been made.

He hated her enough already.

And yet they were to be married in four days. On Christmas Eve.

"What are you doing out here in the snow?" Her father's voice cut the silence.

Elizabeth opened her eyes and turned to see her father striding toward her.

"You mustn't become ill. We can't have that. You are the only thing standing between this family and ruin."

"A few minutes in the snow will hardly send me to my death," she replied quietly.

"Do you realize how serious this situation has become? We are on the verge of losing it all, despite the betrothal agreement. All because of you." Her father's gaze narrowed. "The previous lord and I allowed you your female sentiments by postponing the wedding until you were ready. But no longer. You will marry the new earl before this opportunity escapes us."

A gust of wind tugged at the tawny brown curls she'd failed to tie back. She allowed her father's voice to fade into the background. The wind quickened, bringing heavier flurries of snow. The first low rumble of thunder sounded.

She shuddered at the unusual sound of thunder during a snowstorm. Was it an omen of things to come? When she looked back at the rise of the hill, Lucius was no longer there.

"Elizabeth!" Her father's voice was harsh beside her. "Lord Carrick is arrived. You must go to him."

Elizabeth looked up at her father in wild protest. "Tonight? In this storm?" The land was cloaked in shadow. The wind tore at her hair and flattened her shawl against her chest.

"Aye. Tonight. My debts have already been paid by the former Earl of Carrick, which makes you the new earl's possession now."

"But we've not yet been wed."

"A mere formality. The terms are already arranged and executed. The longer you put this off, the harder it will be. And we cannot risk the new earl pulling out of the agreement."

"Can it not wait until morning at least? He just arrived. Perhaps he wishes time with his sisters."

Her father shook his head. " 'Tis done. Let it be over with. Off you go."

"Will you not go with me?"

He shook his head. "You are best rid of me as I am of you."

His words brought tears to her eyes that were quickly slapped away by the wind. She should have been used to the bite of his tongue and his neglect. The only time he was ever pleasant to her was when he was in his cups, or gaming, and he was neither of those things now.

Elizabeth drew herself up. Her father's debts had been paid. His life was renewed. For her, the payment of that debt had only just begun. Her father's mind was made up. "I shall go, if that's what you desire." Her voice was uneven and she had to steady it before she continued. "Might I at least take the wagon?"

He nodded. "If you're quick about it. I want Farnsworth to return with the horses before the snow gets any deeper."

Elizabeth nodded numbly as she moved back toward the structure that was her home no longer.

It took Elizabeth's father's only remaining servant, his steward, a short while to pack her clothing into her trunk and strap it to the wagon. With a final nod, her father sent her out into the darkness to travel the short distance to Midwick Manor.

If only I could put this off until tomorrow. Or forever. Elizabeth drew a ragged breath and willed her heart to slow as the wagon pulled to a stop in the drive of Midwick Manor. A single stable boy came out to assist her. The young boy and her father's steward settled her trunk near the door. With a bow, Farnsworth returned to the wagon and set the horses in motion, leaving her standing beside the stable boy.

Elizabeth held her tears in check. It would not help her

to spill them now. Her father cared nothing for her. His delivery of her unto her bridegroom was proof of that. She suspected that by the end of the week, instead of attending her wedding, he would be on his way to Edinburgh and the nearest gaming house to spend what little remained of her wedding price.

Drawing in a breath, Elizabeth steadied herself. Her father and Huntingdon Hall were her past. The doorway leading inside Midwick Manor was her future, and she would make the best of the situation. She was away from her father's gaming, and his foolishness. She should find relief in that fact and make the very best of the situation at hand.

She had to succeed here. Lucius had to marry her. If he did not… She forced the thought away. There was no going back for her.

"Are ye ready tae go inside?" the stable boy asked, breaking into her thoughts.

"Oh aye, forgive me. I was just taking a moment to gather myself." Elizabeth ran a hand through the wild tangle that was her hair. Her fingers tugged against the knots the wind had created. She hadn't even had time to prepare herself. Her father had been in such a hurry to get her away from Huntingdon Hall. She frowned into the darkness. Her old gown, tangled curls. What a beguiling bride she made. Assuming Lucius…Lord Carrick…would have her.

She straightened. He would accept her. He had to. She'd been waiting her whole life to have the kind of home she'd always wanted. Mustering her resolve, Elizabeth nodded to the young man beside her. He opened the door, then waved her inside.

"Wait here, milady. I'll get Marie for ye."

Elizabeth waited in silence for several long moments before a portly woman with silver-brown hair and rosy cheeks hustled toward her from the back of the house. "Oh goodness," the woman said, her kind eyes growing wide. " 'Tis you!"

"I do apologize for this inconvenience. My father felt it urgent I come to you this evening." Elizabeth gripped the handle on her trunk. She lifted the edge, then dragged it farther inside.

"The master is home, he is. Though I'm nae certain this was the wisest way tae—"

"I'll take care of this, Marie."

The familiar male voice was hard and cool. A shiver went down Elizabeth's spine. The trunk slipped from her hand and hit the stone floor with a thud that echoed in the deathly stillness of the hallway.

Marie bowed, then with a last look of concern fled the scene.

Elizabeth dropped her gaze to the floor, to the black boots not two feet from her. She'd known this moment would come. She'd dreaded seeing Lucius again after they'd parted on such bad terms. She'd rehearsed in her mind so many ways she should respond to him: with cool aloofness in one scenario, with meekness in another. Neither of those practiced responses came to her now.

He was dressed in a dark tunic and breeches that were slightly rumpled, as though he too had not had time to refresh himself since his arrival home. It took everything she had to look him in the face.

"Are you so eager to marry the lord of this manor that you had to come tonight?" His words were harsh.

Looking at him now, at the barely concealed anger that flashed in his eyes, she knew that time had not dulled the way in which they'd parted five years earlier. "My father insisted."

"Well, at least you've learned how to obey in the years we've been apart." He glared at her.

"Don't you dare look at me that way. I'm not entirely at fault for how we parted." Elizabeth started pacing as her fear vanished. "Or for the situation we find ourselves in now. You could have…"

His hand gently clasped her wrist, stalling her movements. "I could have what?" His tone was soft.

Heat rose to her cheeks. The tension between them became palpable. You could have fought for me. She met his gaze directly. "It's in the past." She was spared from explaining further when a ruckus erupted from the ladies' parlor. Squeals of delight and laughter mixed with the scamper of feet. Lucius's fingers vanished from her wrist. A moment later she found herself enveloped in the arms of his five sisters.

"You're here!" Heather cried, breaking out of her usual shyness. "Let me take your cloak." The young woman had the garment off her shoulders before Elizabeth could even agree.

"You're just in time for supper." Camellia smiled. "Please, sit by me, Miss Huntingdon. Tell me everything you know of…well, anyone! We've had so few visitors in the past months."

Rose squeezed Elizabeth's arm affectionately. "Having both you and our brother here will make everything better for all of us." At Elizabeth's doubtful look, she added, "I know it to be the truth. You'll see."

Elizabeth could only nod in reply. Why were they all being so nice to her? She'd been so worried that they would feel threatened or even resentful of her coming to take over the manor when the older girls were coming of age to do so themselves. She drew a sharp breath as she studied Rose's face. There was no animosity there, only relief.

The youngest girl, Lily, put her hand in Elizabeth's and offered her an innocent smile. "Our new sister has arrived, just as we requested," she said, her tone filled with awe.

Instead of the harsh response Elizabeth had expected, Lucius smiled.

He ruffled Lily's curly hair. "And here I thought you all as guileless as lambs. Instead you're plotting to snare me."

In the presence of his sisters, Lucius had transformed back into the man she remembered from her youth. He was alive again. All coolness had vanished. Or so she thought, until in the next heartbeat he turned to her. "We are not done with this conversation. Join us for supper, but after that you and I shall talk in private. Agreed?"

She nodded. It wasn't important that he love her, only that she be allowed to remain. "I'll not go home."

"We'll see about that," he said, then surprised her by offering his arm. After a slight hesitation, she placed her fingers on his forearm. She was suddenly conscious of the solid warmth of his body, the narrowed intensity of his eyes as he studied her. His anger vanished, replaced by a momentary smile.

Her breath stilled. She remembered that smile, the one that had warmed her clear to her toes and had made her reckless. Elizabeth flexed, then relaxed, her fingers on his arm, praying the sizzling sensation he'd sparked in her would dissipate. It didn't. But the knowledge of her continued attraction to the man steadied her resolve as she allowed him to lead her to the hall. She had no choice but to marry him. She'd already been sold to the Earl of Carrick to pay for her father's mistakes. She had no choice but to give this man her body as was his right by marriage, but her mind, her will, and most definitely her heart were her own.

All through the meal Lucius had been conscious of a change in Elizabeth. Something within her had shifted, taken on strength over the years they'd been separated. It bothered him, though he wasn't sure why.

Her delicate features had become more pronounced over the last five years. As a young girl she'd been attractive, with her wide brown eyes dominating her face. Now, she was a true Scottish beauty. The evening's candlelight revealed a heart-shaped face with a delicate jaw. Her lips were full and darkly sensual. Her tawny hair was a riot that looked as though it refused to be tamed. For a heartbeat he was glad to be free of his Templar oath of chastity.

Lucius frowned at the thought. Elizabeth might be beautiful, but she was not for him. He set his goblet on the table and rose to his feet. "Miss Huntingdon, Elizabeth, we must talk."

Elizabeth nodded as she stood, then bade his sisters good night. She drifted toward him, her posture rigid, her chin held high. A pillar of strength in a delicate package. He led her through the hall and into the solar. At the doorway he stopped. This room had always been his father's private chamber. The furnishings were just as they'd been when Lucius had left. For a moment he forgot all about Elizabeth and drifted into the room.

His father's desk. His fingers traced the polished surface. Behind the desk stood a shelf filled with the estate's accounts. To the left of the desk leaned a cane. His father's favorite. Lucius clamped his jaw against a rising tide of unwanted emotions. The man was gone. As was his brother. The estate and the welfare of his sisters were in his hands now.

He twisted back to Elizabeth. "Sit," he commanded, and directed her to the elaborately carved wooden bench near the shuttered window. He stood before her, towering over her. "I have no wish to marry you," he said bluntly. "As I am sure you have no wish to marry me."

She studied her hands, folded neatly in her lap. "In that you are wrong, my lord. My father and your brother have determined our fate. There is no going back."

"God's teeth!" Lucius erupted. "You'll cry off this betrothal at once."

Her gaze shot to his face. "It is impossible."

"Why? You don't care about me. 'Tis Marcus you loved." She paled ever so slightly, no doubt at the mention of her lost lover.

"You know little of my heart." She shifted her gaze to a point over his shoulder. "If the marriage does not occur, my father will be ruined."

He frowned. "How can that be?"

Again her gaze met his, and this time he saw something that hadn't been there before: fear. "Your family paid my father's debts. There is no possible way for us to pay you back. And no other future for me."

He turned away from her and walked behind his father's desk. His desk now, he amended. "Keep the money. I don't need it."

"That cannot be done."

" 'Tis a business arrangement. We shall make another one where you cry off and I make a gift of the funds to your family."

"If this marriage does not go through, I'll be destitute," she said, her voice barely above a whisper.

He hardened his heart to the sweet sound of her voice, which made his every nerve stand on end. "I don't care what becomes of you, just as you did not care about my feelings that day in the garden when I caught you and Marcus together."

"You saw what you wanted to see. Marcus surprised me. I did not return his kiss." She clutched her hands together, yet he noted how her fingers trembled regardless.

"You appeared to be enjoying yourself."

She remained silent.

"I would have stayed away from here forever."

She brought her gaze to his. "Then why did you come back?"

"Because I care what happens to my sisters."

"So do I." She straightened, and all her nervousness vanished. "You might think I have nothing to offer you in this marriage, but I do. I have many connections with the local clans. I can use those connections to help your sisters make agreeable matches. Without such guidance, they will likely end up in miserable situations or not married at all, and become old maids. Is that what you want for them?"

Cold, dark fury ate away at him as he glared at the woman who had fallen for his brother instead of him.

Despite his angry assault, her features softened. "No one asked you if you wanted this, Lucius, I understand that. No one asked me either. Marcus and my father swore to honor the pact. Not us."

He released a harsh breath. "So what are we to do? How do we undo what others have done?"

"We honor the betrothal."

"That is not acceptable."

"You've just arrived home. Will you not think on this for even one night? Please, Lucius, I beg of you."

"Is that why you came tonight instead of tomorrow? To force me into this decision all the sooner?"

Elizabeth paled. "I came because my father made me. As I am of no further use to him, he wanted me gone."

Lucius frowned. Obviously much had changed between

Elizabeth and her father since her mother had died six years ago. "Very well," he said. "We will leave things as they are for tonight. But in the next four days I shall make you see all the reasons this marriage should not go through." He turned away, thinking he had the last words.

"And I have four days to make you see it should."

Chapter Three

The blackguard has come home. Horatio Carr thrummed his fingers against the stout table in the common room of the Beardsman Inn, where he'd been forced to lodge. He should have been in the master's chamber at Midwick Manor instead of at this lowly inn on the outskirts of Newcastleton.

Why hadn't the French eliminated Lucius as they had his brother Peter? Better the French take the young heir than that the killing fall to him. But now he'd be forced into the deed if he wanted what should have rightfully been his: Midwick Manor and the earldom.

All around him the din of many conversations added a sense of confusion. He pressed his fingers against his temples in an attempt to gather his thoughts. He needed a plan.

Horatio frowned down into the empty mug that had only a short while ago been filled with ale. How could he force the boy back toward the Templars? If his nephew renounced the title, everything would fall into place. Then Horatio could begin his future as the Earl of Carrick. At the thought, his chest warmed. It had been so long since he had the kind of respect he deserved. How could being born a mere two minutes behind his brother separate the heir from the spare? Damn the system that had denied him his due.

Horatio increased the pressure of his fingers against his forehead. He'd already stolen away most of the staff in hopes the estate would cease to function. He hadn't expected the servants who'd remained to increase their efforts tenfold to keep that from happening. Though the estate was not thriving, it limped along. He could afford to cripple the estate during the winter season. But he would have to succeed by the growing season, or the failure of the estate would become his problem.

Time was of the essence here.

And in order to succeed, he needed another tactic, something far more devastating, something that would cut the young pup to the quick. Then an idea formed. The perfect solution to Horatio's problem. He knew Lucius's weakness. It was the reason he'd returned home.

His sisters.

Horatio closed his eyes, trying to block out the laughter of the woman sitting behind him and the shouts of the two men near the fire who wrestled each other like they were playing out of doors. The thump of a body against a wooden table made him startle.

He stood and backed into the shadows of the chamber as other men joined the fray. Horatio watched the ruckus, and as he did, his plan took on dimension. He needed at least two of these thugs as part of his plan.

The girls were the key. Lucius would return to the Templars or die. Horatio cared not which.

He pressed himself against the rough stone wall in the shadows. His cheeks heated, his fists curled and uncurled as hatred seethed green and evil within him. He would use the girls to get everything he wanted. Everything.

ॐ

Lucius stretched in the chair he'd slept in by the hearth in the great hall, trying to work the kinks out of his neck. He'd slept in worse conditions, but never in his own home. He had a perfectly good bed waiting for him upstairs, yet he hadn't been able to bring himself to sleep in it or the chamber that had belonged to his father, and to Marcus after that. There were too many memories lingering abovestairs, memories he wasn't prepared to confront just yet.

Lucius stood and stretched again and noted the light seeping through the shutters was brighter than normal. He crossed the chamber and threw the shutters open. A blast of cold air greeted him, as did the sight of the estate blanketed in snow that had fallen during the night.

"Did you sleep well, my lord?"

At the sound of Elizabeth's soft voice, he tensed. "You used to call me Lucius."

"With your permission, I would be delighted to do so once more."

He closed the shutters. "You don't need my permission." A frown tugged at his mouth as he turned to face her. She was dressed in a dark woolen dress and a cloak, and held a second cloak draped over her arm. "You are leaving."

"Nay, you'll not be rid of me so easily, Lucius." She placed an added emphasis on his name. "I've come to take you on an outing." She held the cloak over her arm out to him. "Once you break your fast we'll be on our way."

"Where?" he asked suspiciously.

She smiled sweetly, and he knew from the days of their youth that the glint of determination in her eyes meant he wouldn't get anything more from her until he agreed.

He accepted the cloak. "If I do this, will you leave then?"

Her smile slipped a notch. "I'll make you no promises. Marie has oats and bacon set out for you in the kitchen."

As she waited for his reply, her gaze moved to the chair he'd slept in and the woolen blanket now lying on the floor alongside it. Her face remained blank, but in her eyes he could see a momentary sadness before she dropped her gaze to her feet.

He'd always been able to read her emotions by her eyes. At the thought he stiffened. What did he care what emotion she was experiencing, especially on his behalf? Elizabeth had betrayed him, and here was no forgiving that. He tossed the cloak over his shoulders and pushed past her, heading toward the kitchen. "Very well. Let's get this charade over with, so then you can leave."

Before his sisters had risen from their beds, he and Elizabeth were out of doors. She led him to the stable, where two horses were saddled and ready for them. Elizabeth moved to the mounting block and easily slipped onto the back of her horse.

Lucius frowned, irritated by the knowledge she didn't need his assistance to mount. Was she avoiding his touch? Or was she making a show of her independence?

He mounted his horse and forced the thoughts away. He could not afford to care about her feelings or her motives. His presence on this outing was merely a means to get her to leave, nothing more.

As she turned toward the door, he noticed a dark bundle attached to the back of her horse. "What's in the satchel?" he asked as he followed her.

She stopped her horse and turned to him. "Gifts from you to your tenants."

"What are you about?"

She ignored his tartness. "You need to meet your people. They are eager to meet you. And since it is customary for the lord of the manor to deliver coins to the crofters and servants at Christmastide, I asked Hadwell if you could do both at the same time. He agreed and gave me the funds."

His gaze narrowed. "You are overstepping your authority."

"As the future mistress of this estate, I must think of its people."

He drew a deep breath. "You are not mistress here yet, and will never be if I have my way." At the hurt in her eyes, he softened his tone. "Besides, coins are to be dispersed on Saint Stephen's feast day, the day after Christmas."

She held her chin high. "It would better serve your people to have the coins early this year, for they have suffered much by the loss of your father and brother."

A rush of pain moved through him at her words. He hated to admit she was right. Those of his people who remained at the estate deserved kindness this year more than any other. At the mention of his tenants, his thoughts wandered to those who'd left. Where had they gone and what was their condition? The borderlands could be a treacherous place for clan members living on their own.

Determined to get this outing over with, he set his horse in motion, driving the beast into the foot-deep snow. Regardless of whether it was his idea to go to the crofters or Elizabeth's, he did need to talk with them and figure out what had happened to those who'd left the estate. It was his duty to see to their safety, no matter what his uncle had offered them to leave.

Pale blue skies stretched overhead. The sun bathed the snow in sparkling iridescence that lent further peacefulness to the scene as they progressed to the south. The rhythm of the horses' hooves in the ice-crusted snow was the only sound greeting them as they made their way across the fallow fields. They rode in silence, with only the sound of the harness jingling to fill the space until they came to the first crofter cottage bordering the edge of the loch.

"Bentner and his lady live here with their five children," she reminded him as they dismounted. She untied the satchel and handed it to him. "For you to disperse as you see fit."

He accepted the heavy bag and opened it up to see not only a bag of coins at the top, but several packages wrapped in linen and tied with twine. "What's in the packages?"

She lifted her chin and a hint of a challenge came into her eyes. "Marie thought you should share a ham with them for their Yuletide celebrations."

He raised a brow. "She did, did she?"

Elizabeth nodded, but her gaze searched the area near the croft cottage instead of settling on him. Her inability to look people in the face gave her away every time she told a lie. Lucius bit back a smile and headed for the door. "It was a good suggestion, whoever's idea it was," Lucius said.

After a jam tart and three cups of tea, Lucius and Elizabeth made their good-byes and headed for the southern tip of the estate. "Does Jacob Insley still live on this patch of land?" Lucius asked as they neared the Insley cottage.

"Aye," Elizabeth replied. "He and his new wife, Jayne, are there."

Lucius smiled at the memory of Jacob Insley. He'd been a frequent visitor at Midwick Manor when Lucius was young. The two men had become friends regardless of their rank, and Lucius was eager to see his old companion once more. They were riding toward the cottage when they saw a tall man with shockingly red hair pacing back and forth in front of the door. "Jacob?" Lucius called as both he and Elizabeth dismounted and hurried forward.

It took a moment before recognition dawned on the young man's face, but when it did he ran to them and clasped Lucius's arm. "Praise the saints ye are safely with us again, milord."

At Jacob's pale face, the wind suddenly felt a little

cooler. "What's wrong?"

" 'Tis my Jayne. She's been laboring with our second child fer a day. The midwife told me tae come outside and walk around the house backwards tae try tae help alleviate her pain."

"I'll go see what I can do to help," Elizabeth said as she hurried inside the cottage.

"Would you like some company on your jaunt?" Lucius said when they were alone.

"Aye. That I would," Jacob said. "For a moment there, I feared ye were the English."

Lucius frowned. "Are the raids that frequent?"

"Aye. They know the country is weakened with the Bruce gone and his child on the throne."

Lucius sighed. "I've been so caught up in the Templars' troubles with the French that I hadn't heard…" He let his words trail off. It was no excuse. He was a landowner now and responsible for the safety of his people. "When was the last raid? And how many men did they have?"

"Last week they came across the border west of here and torched the MacKinley land, and stole their cattle. George MacKinley died, but his son Silas and their men managed tae fend off the English before anyone else was killed."

Lucius kept his expression neutral, though inside, alarm rippled though him. The English usually only stole cattle. That they'd killed George MacKinley indicated they might be testing the border's defenses for another, larger attack.

Before he could respond to Jacob, the door of the croft

opened and Elizabeth stepped back into the snow. A worried expression brought shadows to her eyes. "Jayne's labor is harder than it should be. The babe is large, but it's more than that. She's nervous about the raid that happened last week. Mistress Grayson fears unless Jayne feels safe enough to deliver the babe, they both might die."

Elizabeth met his gaze. "Jayne would be better served if she had men to guard her. But that is your decision to make." Elizabeth's gaze dipped to her toes as though she feared what his response might be.

Instead of making the decision for him as she had about this trip, she'd given him the chance to decide Jayne's fate, even though there really was no choice. "Jacob, go tell your wife that reinforcements from Midwick are on their way. After the baby is born, I want you all to move in to the manor house with us. Jayne and the baby will be well cared for there. Marie and Hadwell will see to that."

Jacob's eyes misted. "Thank you, milord."

As Jacob disappeared into the cottage, Elizabeth turned to Lucius. "There's no one at Midwick Manor to guard anyone."

"Which is why I'm going back to the Bentners to ask for their help." He drew his sword and pressed the hilt of the weapon into Elizabeth's hands.

"I don't know how to use a sword."

"Let's hope you won't have to. I'll be back soon." He strode to his horse, leaving Elizabeth staring down at the weapon.

Chapter Four

Lucius arrived back at the Insleys' cottage a short while later with Hamish Bentner and his wife. The three of them, along with Elizabeth, took turns watching the approach from the border as Jacob reassured his wife that they were safe from harm. If the English chose this moment to attack, Lucius doubted the four of them would have any chance of fending them off. But Jayne didn't need to know that.

After a long and exhausting day of waiting, a soft wail echoed from inside the cottage, followed by a second wail that mixed with a mother's cry of relief.

"Congratulations." Lucius smiled at Jacob as he emerged from the house. Jacob had been at Jayne's side for hours, and the man appeared as tired and worn out as if it were he who'd given birth.

Jacob smiled, and suddenly his tiredness vanished. "Praise the saints," he said, and clapped Lucius on the shoulder, his voice filed with pride. "I'm a father again!"

Instead of sharing in the man's excitement, Lucius paused. "You could have lost her and the baby."

Joy brightened Jacob's eyes. "There's that risk in everything we do, my friend. 'Tis the good things that happen that get us through the bad." His smile widened. "Ye helped make this outcome possible, and I thank ye for that. Good comes in turns, and now it's yer turn fer the good to come yer way."

It was not what Jacob had said, but the passion in his words, that brought a sense of heaviness to Lucius's chest. He deserved good? He didn't believe that.

He deserved to be punished for turning his back on Marcus when his brother needed him most. If only he'd been there when the English had raided. Maybe then… Lucius turned toward his horse, wanting desperately to escape. What? His friend? His own thoughts? His belief that he didn't deserve more than the pain that his life had been filled with?

Fairy tales and happy endings were something he knew a great deal about. His mother had spun a thousand stories in the evenings before the fire for his brothers and sisters, each tale grander and more far-fetched than the last. For years, he'd actually believed his mother's tales.

He'd been a young man of sixteen when reality had hit, and hit hard. He'd fallen in love. He hadn't meant to. It just happened one day while he was walking along the loch with his best friend. In the late afternoon sun, he'd taken her hand, glanced into her eyes, and a thrill he'd never experienced before moved through him—a thrill he felt suddenly was necessary to his life.

He'd meant to tell her how he felt, but the words never seemed to come. He tried to show her, but his actions were thwarted when Marcus intruded and captured his beloved's attention.

Then one dark, dreary morning, he'd seen the truth in his brother's eyes. He'd fallen for the girl as well. A final stab to his heart had been when he'd caught the two of them together in a passionate embrace in the garden. As he watched their betrayal, all of his hopes and dreams shattered. From then on he'd stopped believing in anything good, and he'd run away, just as he was tempted to do now.

But running was no longer possible. His sisters needed him. And he'd learned a hard, cruel lesson: running didn't stop the pain. Instead, it only made it worse. The best he could do was dredge up something to salvage the situation.

Lucius turned back to Jacob with his expression carefully blank. His people needed his help. Perhaps that's where this goodness Jacob prophesied would come into being, but that didn't mean any of it would spill his way. Experience had taught him that dreams of happy endings were a useless waste of time.

"Before we pack up Jayne and the children to take all of you back to Midwick Manor, might I ask you one more thing?" The sound of his voice echoed in the silence of the late-afternoon air. "If things are so good here at Midwick, then why have all the servants deserted us?"

Jacob's face turned solemn. " 'Tis yer uncle who's behind it. He's payin' them twice their yearly salary tae leave and he's a tellin' them stories about how ye changed. That the Templars turned ye into a merciless beast."

Lucius stilled. "Did he approach you?"

Jacob nodded. "I could see past his lies. He's tryin' to hurt ye by takin' away yer help. He's made no secret of the fact he wants the earldom, or that he wants ye out of the way in order tae get it."

Lucius schooled his features into a hard mask, fighting the pain of yet another betrayal. "Horatio expects the law of inheritance to change solely for his purposes?"

Jacob met his gaze. "Don't let yer uncle win this battle. I know ye've got it in ye tae fight. I remember that much from our youth." He rubbed his jaw as though remembering one of the many punches Lucius had landed there during their mock battles.

"Enough of this morbidity. You've got happier things to celebrate. Go prepare your family for travel. I'll get the wagon ready."

"Thank ye, my friend, milord." Jacob took two steps toward the cottage door, then stopped and turned back around. "I meant what I said. Yer a good man. I'll never forget what ye did fer us this day."

At Lucius's nod, Jacob hastened into the cottage, leaving him alone with his thoughts. Fight. Lucius tipped his head back and breathed a heavy sigh. He'd become a fighter for other people's causes over the years. Could he do the same for himself? Could he gather his people and train them in the ways of battle he'd learned with the Templars so they could withstand not only his uncle, but the English as well?

He had ties to the Bentner and Insley clans. Then there were the MacKinleys. Would they join him in this cause? There was only one way to find out. He'd ride for the MacKinleys' land first thing on the morrow.

In the meanwhile, he'd take stock of what weapons and defenses his brother and father had left him. They'd lived on the border between Scotland and England all their lives.

Everyone in the borderlands had to be prepared for invasion at any time. There were bound to be defenses they'd gathered in the years he'd been gone.

His sole job now was to see that his sisters and his people were safe.

Lucius frowned. Something bad hovered on the horizon. He'd felt nothing but tension in the air today. Whether that tension came from his uncle or the English, he wasn't certain.

One lesson he'd learned from the Templars, and learned well, was to be prepared for anything.

That was at least something he could focus on to keep his mind from other things.

Elizabeth pulled her cloak more tightly around herself as she stepped outside Midwick Manor. She still felt unsettled even though Jacob, Jayne and the babe, and their young daughter Maybel were now safely tucked into a bedchamber abovestairs. Perhaps a stroll would help relieve the unease that came from her own uncertain future.

Elizabeth headed toward the loch and the icy fringe that had settled along the shoreline. Now that the excitement of the day had faded, her own troubles left her edgy and, if she was honest with herself, fearful. Her life would change in a dramatic way in three days' time.

She breathed out a column of frosty air that quickly

vanished. How would she ever convince Lucius to go through with their marriage? She wasn't the kind of woman who got what she wanted through tricks or ploys. Nay, he would either accept her or reject her. And rejection seemed the more likely of the two.

And if he rejected her, she would be alone in this world with no one to rely on and nowhere to turn. Slowly, she walked in silent contemplation, until she realized where her feet had taken her. She paused as a tall, winged statue blocked the late-afternoon sun from her eyes. The angel's mildew-stained hands were outstretched in greeting, yet the statue's carved eyes were upon her, silently condemning her for invading the solace of the cemetery. Two steps more took her past the angel and to the foot of Marcus's grave.

A soft rustle sounded behind her.

"Do you miss him so very much?"

Elizabeth turned to face Lucius. For a split second she saw the boy who'd once lived behind those dark eyes. He used to laugh with her and talk with her about any number of things. His smile had seemed ever present.

He was not smiling now. "Do you miss him?" Lucius repeated.

"Some days." It was all she could say past the lump in her throat.

He nodded and came to stand beside her. "What was he like before he…" His words trailed off, but she knew what he was asking.

"He was happy, as Marcus always was. Nothing ever seemed to bother him." She couldn't bring herself to tell him about how Hadwell had found him upon the battlefield with a sword through his heart. Marcus had died defending his family and his country.

He'd had so few men that day when he went to attack the English. Yet Marcus felt it was a risk worth taking to save even one person he loved.

Elizabeth would do the same to save the family she so desperately wanted with the man before her. She'd been so close to that once. She'd known something was changing between Lucius and herself. But once Marcus started paying attention to her, his brother stopped looking at her at all.

Then he'd left without giving her a chance to explain the kiss he'd witnessed. He'd never even said good-bye. Elizabeth closed her eyes, trying to block the memory of the day Lucius left her for what she'd thought was forever. He'd always been her friend, yet she'd hidden from him how difficult things had become for her at Huntingdon Hall after her mother died. He had no idea how lonely she'd become or the misery she'd endured with no money to pay servants or even put food on the table. That's when her father started selling off their possessions.

"Elizabeth?" Lucius's voice jerked her back to the present. "You looked sad there for a moment. What is it?"

She opened her eyes and met his gaze. She could lie to him, put on the mantle of the grieving fiancée, but she had no stomach for it today. "My regrets have more to do with you than Marcus."

His eyes darkened. "Me? Why?" Bitterness lingered in his words.

Elizabeth swallowed the lump lodging like old dust in her throat. Could she tell him? Could she risk it all now? Open the old hurts and wounds that had been festering for so long?

She straightened. The time for fear was past. She was tired of lying and pretending. She was tired of being afraid. Perhaps the two of them could bridge the divide she'd wedged between them by accepting Marcus's advances instead of forcing him away. "Why did you leave Midwick Manor?"

"There was nothing left for me here. The Templars needed me."

Elizabeth felt tears sting her eyes. "Lucius, I needed you."

"It certainly didn't look it."

She shook her head. "Nay, you don't understand. Marcus kissed me. I was surprised, didn't know what to do. You assumed—"

"I saw the look in my brother's eyes. He'd fallen in love with you."

"But I had not fallen in love with him. Why did you not look into my eyes? You would have known the truth." Elizabeth took a deep breath. She had nothing to lose and everything to gain in the next heartbeat. "I have always loved you."

He remained silent, but she could see the thump of his pulse in his jaw. He turned his gaze to the grave at their feet. "But why…?" he finally said, almost to himself.

"I didn't get a chance to speak with you. You were gone the next day." She paused. "I waited months for you to return. You didn't."

Silence settled between them. "I miss him," Lucius finally said. "I could have come back to see him at any time, but I was always too busy with one Templar cause or another. After Peter's death, I missed Marcus all the more. And even then, I stayed away. If only I'd come home, maybe then he would still be here. Maybe I could have saved him from the English."

"No one could have saved him. The battle was swift. We had no time to gather the clans. Ten good men died that day, and the clans have been suffering since. The border is weak. I think that in part is why your uncle had such an easy time sending the servants away. They were scared with no one to protect them."

"I'm here to protect all of you now." His brow furrowed. "But even I cannot protect these lands alone."

"You aren't alone. We are all here, waiting for guidance, waiting to build a new future with you."

"Is that why you're here, Elizabeth? To build a new future?"

The tears she'd been fighting spilled over her lashes and onto her cheeks. *I have no future without you.* She wanted to say the words, but they lodged in her throat. Instead, she stepped toward him and took his face between her palms. She pressed up on her toes and brought her lips to his, ever so gently, before pulling away. "The future awaits," she whispered against his lips.

Lucius did not kiss her back. "I need time, Elizabeth, to sort things out."

"You have three days, Lucius," Elizabeth said. And on

those words, she hurried back to the manor.

When the first rays of sunlight woke Elizabeth the next morning, her thoughts immediately returned to last night. Had Lucius thought about their moments beside Marcus's grave as much as she had? Lucius had been unresponsive to her profession of love and to her kiss. Was all hope for a future together lost? Or had the night given him the time he'd claimed he needed to think about their situation?

Only seeing him in the flesh would tell her what she needed to know. But it was the hope of change that fueled her movements as she dressed then hastened downstairs to the great hall. She gazed about the chamber only to find Marie tending to a pot hanging over the fire in the hearth.

"Excuse me, Marie. Where might I find Lord Carrick? Is he about yet?"

Marie tapped her spoon on the edge of the kettle before turning to face her. "I'm sorry, my lady. He's already gone."

"Where?" she asked in a pleading whisper.

Marie shrugged and offered an understanding smile. "He said nothing, only to expect him later because of the snow."

"More snow?" Elizabeth swallowed her disappointment as she moved to the shuttered window on the opposite side of the large room. She pulled up the latch and swung the shutter out to see snow lying three feet deep against the side of the manor. Beyond lay a pure white carpet with no hint of shrubs or landscape. Even the loch lay covered in a sheet of white. The skeletons of oak and rowan trees that lined the loch's eastern shore glistened beneath a layer of ice and snow.

Abovestairs, she could hear the girls' excited chatter as one by one they drifted down the stairs, until they all stood at the window.

"I've never seen so much snow." Iris, who showed no signs of her usual grumpiness, leaned through the open window and breathed in a deep breath of the cool, crisp air.

"It's lovely!" Camellia exclaimed with a bright smile.

"Let's go outside." Lily tugged on Elizabeth's skirt. "Please?"

"It's two days until Christmastide. We must gather the greens and decorate." Heather looked at Elizabeth expectantly.

"It's two days until you and our brother are to be married." Rose bent down and lifted Lily into her arms. "We need to prepare."

"We can do both. Play outside and gather greens." Lily nodded, sending her curls bobbing around her flushed cheeks.

"Please, Elizabeth, say we can," they begged in unison.

When she held up a hand, silence fell. "Break your fast first," she told them. "Once you have dressed in your boots and warmest cloaks, hats, and mittens, then you can go outside. Understood?"

Five girls nodded enthusiastically and hurried from the chamber, dancing along the hallway toward the stairs, talking loudly, and making wild plans for all the fun they'd have in the snow.

It seemed like only a few moments before they were gathered once more in the hall dressed for their adventure out of doors. Elizabeth had used her time to find an ax and a pair of shears, along with a basket for gathering the greens. She knew exactly where she would take the girls—to the woods that served as a border between Midwick Manor and Huntingdon Hall. Holly, ivy, and mistletoe grew there in abundance.

They left the manor through the kitchen door facing the open terrain covered in white. Once outside the younger girls seemed more excited about playing in the snow than finding decorations. Rose and Camellia agreed to indulge them for a time, and they put their decorating mission aside temporarily.

While the young girls scurried about in the snow, Rose and Camellia made a large snowball, then a smaller one, before putting them together into a snowman greeting visitors to the kitchen door. Heather and Iris lay in the snow, making a host of snow angels. Lily gathered and threw snowballs at everyone.

Elizabeth ducked to avoid taking a snowball in the head. Caught up in the girls' good humor, she swept up a handful of snow and sent it flying. It hit Camellia square in the back. The sixteen-year-old's eyes widened as a smile wreathed her face, and suddenly Elizabeth found herself the center of all the girls' snowballs. Her dramatic responses to each hit and miss, and her own missiles, kept them all laughing for much of the morning. Finally, when the girls had had enough, they followed Elizabeth up a hill for several hundred feet to the top of a ridge. The ridge stood no more than five feet wide, but the narrow sliver of land had always served as a dividing line between the two estates. It had been one of her favorite places to come as a child and wait for Lucius to join her for an afternoon of frolicking and games.

"You can see Midwick Manor and Huntingdon Hall from here," Lily exclaimed.

Elizabeth shook off the memory and looked down on the place she used to call home. A pang of sadness filled her. This ridge was a divide between her future and her past.

"Do you miss your home?" Rose asked quietly beside her.

Elizabeth swallowed thickly and looked up at the tall blonde. "I do and I don't. It's hard to explain."

"I'm old enough to remember how things used to be between you and Lucius," Rose said. Her light eyes held a note of sympathy.

"That was a long time ago. Much has happened since then."

Rose shook her head. "Perhaps between you and Lucius, but not with us girls. You've always been our friend, and when we learned you were to be our sister, we were all so happy." She turned her gaze to the younger girls, who still threw snowballs at each other. "Lily never knew our mother, since she died giving birth to her. Iris and Heather only have faint memories. They need you."

"And you and Camellia? Why would you accept me so readily when you two have been in charge here for so long?"

Rose met her gaze. "We love our family, but we both want to find a family of our own someday."

Elizabeth's cheeks warmed. She understood that sentiment all too well. "Looks like we have some decorating to do if we are going to get the hall ready for not only Christmastide, but a wedding celebration."

Lily dropped her snowball and her small hand reached up to touch Elizabeth's sleeve. "You'll stay with us forever, right?"

Elizabeth smiled and covered the gloved fingers with her own. "You all are everything I've ever dreamed of in this life. My home is Midwick Manor for as long as your brother will have me."

"We want you to stay forever," Lily said wistfully.

"Only your brother can determine that."

Heather leaped from one edge of the ridge to the other. "Then let's decorate the house and make things so beautiful, he can't help but want you to stay."

If only it were that simple. "We'd better get busy then." Elizabeth forced excitement into her voice as she headed for the holly bush off to her left.

The girls raced ahead of her along the edge of the ridge and busied themselves collecting greens and pinecones and pulling mistletoe down from where it had climbed up into the branches of the trees, until the basket was filled to overflowing. Only then did they scour the area in search of the perfect tree with which to make their Yule log. The girls raced along the long, flat ridge, heading farther south until they came to a stop in front of a tall tree that grew just off the side of the flattened area.

"This is it!" Iris exclaimed.

"It's perfect," the other girls echoed.

"It will definitely keep burning for the twelve days of Christmastide," Camellia said with awe in her voice.

Elizabeth carried the ax with her to the tree. She stopped before the girls' selection and braced herself on the incline. The tree was big, and would no doubt be heavy once she chopped it down. If she could chop it down, she amended, eyeing the thick trunk. "Perhaps we should wait for your brother to help with the tree."

"At your service, my lady," came a voice from behind her.

"Lucius!" Lily cried, and threw herself into his arms.

Elizabeth startled. They'd been so absorbed in their gathering and tree hunting that they hadn't seen his approach. And he'd come from the direction of her father's house. Why?

She took a step toward him, but the uneven ground knocked her off balance. She dropped the ax as she tried to regain her footing. Instead, she slipped, fell, then tumbled down the ridge. Trees dashed in and out of her vision. A woodsy smell invaded her senses. Pain erupted against her temple. The edges of her vision turned black and everything started to spin.

Chapter Five

"Elizabeth!"

Lucius reached out to grab her, but he was too late. She tumbled down the eastern side of the ridge on the Huntingdon Hall side.

"Don't you girls move. Do you hear me?" Without waiting for a reply he scrambled after her, falling a few times, dodging trees and fighting the suffocating snow.

Oh, God, not Elizabeth! What have I done?

Lucius tried to hurry, to keep his eyes on her slim form below. His heart pounded in his chest. She lay facedown. Her tawny hair fanned out around her.

"Elizabeth." She was less than ten feet away from him. She moved her arm away from her head.

She is alive.

Then he saw the bloodred snow.

"Lucius," she whispered.

He sank to his knees beside her. "Don't move," he panted, unable to catch his breath. "Lie still. I need to check your wounds." He turned her head slightly. "There's a small gash at your temple. Does your head pain you?"

"I'm dizzy and I feel foolish, but other than that I'm well."

"Let me make certain." He felt over her arms and legs as he had to his brother Templars who'd fallen in battle.

She shifted to her side and reached out to gently grip his hand. She squeezed once before she released him. "Truly, it is just my head."

"Then let's get you back to the manor." At the sound of her weak voice, emotion tightened his chest. She would be all right. She had to be.

He placed his hand at the back of her neck. "I'm going to roll you over. Let me do the work," he urged as he eased her out of the snow to face him. "You're going to be fine." He gathered snow in his palm and gently applied it to the edge of her forehead. She flinched at the cold a moment before she leaned into his touch. "I'm so sorry, Elizabeth. I didn't mean to startle you."

"It was my fault for allowing myself to be distracted by the girls. None of us saw you coming."

He allowed himself a slight smile. "Blame it on the Templars. We were trained to walk silently when approaching the enemy."

Her gaze met his. "Am I the enemy?"

"Nay, Elizabeth. No longer. Let us put that past behind us. Shall we?"

She tried to sit up.

"Rest a moment," he protested, but she ignored him and sat anyway. Lucius leaned back on his haunches and signaled to the girls above that Elizabeth was well.

"I need to get back to the girls." She struggled to stand.

"Let me help you," he said as he stood, then scooped her into his arms.

"I can walk," she protested.

"I insist." He pulled her closer and his body heat

warmed her.

She made no further comment as he carried her back up the hillside to the girls. Once they reached the top, the girls gathered around her.

"Are you hurt?" Camellia asked, her gaze straying to the blood at the side of Elizabeth's head.

"She'll be well once we take her home," Lucius said. "Let's get you all out of the snow."

"But she's bleeding," Lily said with a lisp as she captured Elizabeth's hand in her own smaller one.

"It's nothing serious, my sweet," she said, with a gentle smile.

"Two of you grab the basket of greens and let's go." Lucius tightened his hold on Elizabeth. The girls hurried ahead of them, leaving the two of them alone.

"Why were you at my father's house?" she asked in a voice no more than a whisper. "Were you trying to talk him out of our betrothal?" She stared at him, her eyes filled with a fragile sadness he had never seen there before.

"Your father wasn't home. Farnsworth informed me he's in Edinburgh."

He saw a shimmer of tears glaze her eyes before she turned her face into his chest.

Oh, Lord… Her father was gambling again. Lucius felt almost sick to his stomach at the thought. Elizabeth's father had dumped his daughter in the most inhumane way imaginable, then scurried back to the obsession that would ultimately destroy him. For Lucius had seen for himself the Huntingdon estate had nothing else of value left within it.

"I'll tell you what my father would have said had he been at home. He would say that I am no longer his worry. What happens to me will be of my own choosing."

"And your choice is to be with us?"

She bit her lip and looked past him at the girls, who had reached the rear door of the manor. "I had hoped my kiss last night said it all, but aye, I want to be here with you and your sisters."

He was too stunned by her revelation to respond. Was it his own dreadful assumptions that had set them all on this course? If he'd stayed and confronted Elizabeth or even Marcus, would both his brothers still be alive today?

He paused as they reached the manor at the doorway and drew a sharp breath. Was he making assumptions now about this woman and her plans to situate herself in his life?

"Please set me down." Her voice was soft, but insistent. "I need no further humiliation this day."

He placed her on her feet but kept his hand near the small of her back as she wobbled slightly.

Elizabeth moved a step away from Lucius, inside the doorway and out of his reach. She pushed the heartbreak she felt deep inside her as she cast a final glance at the man she loved.

Lucius now knew everything, her feelings for him and her father's dreadful obsession. He'd no doubt figured out that her father was off gaming with what remained of her bride-price. He'd seen for himself she had nowhere else to go as a result of their family's arrangement. And he didn't seem to care.

Elizabeth turned to go inside when Lucius placed his chilled fingers on her arm. He held her there. Their eyes locked.

A rush of emotion passed over his taut features. "Let me help you, Elizabeth."

She swallowed roughly, then nodded, uncertain what exactly he meant by his words. A part of her was frightened, another part hopeful, as she allowed him to lead her inside the kitchen.

Lucius shooed his sisters out of the chamber. "I'll inform you when Elizabeth is cleaned up."

"Goodness!" Marie swung around from where she stood near the hearth, her hands covered in flour up to her elbows. She turned white at the sight of Elizabeth's head and gown. She wiped the flour from her hands with her apron. "What happened?" Marie grabbed a bowl from the table near the hearth and filled it with water from a pitcher.

"A tree," both Elizabeth and Lucius said in unison.

He picked up a length of clean linen folded on the table, then knelt beside her. After dipping the cloth in water, he gently patted it over her sensitive flesh.

Lucius's touch was warm and excruciatingly intimate as he pushed back her hair from her cheek and dabbed at her jaw and her throat. His hand felt heavy, and her throat fragile and vulnerable. She swallowed. "Is the wound deep?"

"Nay. You are very lucky to have no serious injury."

The color returned to Marie's face. "If the two of ye have the situation in hand, then I'll go check on the girls."

"We're well enough, Marie." Lucius's gaze never left Elizabeth's face as he spoke to the older woman.

Elizabeth's heart accelerated as he dipped the cloth in the water, then caressed her skin from her temple down to her neck. She could feel her skin warming at his nearness. A pulse thrummed at his temple, and she was highly aware of the feathery curve of his half-closed dark lashes.

Did he feel it too? The strange tension that flared between them whenever they touched? She caught the faint fragrance of his scent—cinnamon bark and something deeper, more intimate. She leaned slightly closer and inhaled. She had always loved his unique scent. A heartbeat later she realized what she was doing and straightened.

Could he see her response to him? Would he hold himself back as he had last night by Marcus's graveside? Elizabeth willed herself to breathe slowly, evenly. But even that could not stop the flush rising to her cheeks or the tremble that came to her fingers.

He stood and took the linen he'd used to the table before returning with a clean cloth. He tore it into a thin strip and wrapped it about her head.

"Thank you for being so kind to me."

"Kind?" His laugh held a note of self-deprecation. " 'Tis my fault you slipped."

"When you try to be charming, you truly are."

"Nay, I'm not," he murmured as his lips descended to

hers.

All her senses became focused on the feather-light pressure of his mouth, on the teasing, taunting dalliance of his tongue as it stroked her lips. He shifted toward her and pulled her close, embracing her in a way that made her feel molded to the hard contours of his chest. This moment was everything she'd ever wanted.

His lips slanted more forcefully over hers, and his tongue slid possessively into the heat of her mouth. Her fingers came up to spread across the thickness of his woolen tunic and inched higher…higher…until her arms circled his neck. She pressed herself into his embrace, thrilling in the strength of his arms as they held her.

The kiss she'd given him last night was nothing compared to this kiss. She brought her hand up to tease the hair at the nape of his neck, needing to feel more of him against her.

She drew a deep breath, and it was then that she surfaced enough from her bliss to note the tension in Lucius's shoulders and the stiffness of his posture. Despite the thoroughness of his kiss, he held himself back. Tears pooled in her eyes.

She pulled back with a sob. "Are you kissing me to kiss me, or does this mean what I want it to mean?"

He stared down at her, the line of his cheeks hollow with tension. "Is this not what you wanted?"

His kiss was everything she'd dreamed of. But suddenly it wasn't enough. She didn't want to be alone in her passion. She wanted him to love her in return. "Do your kisses come with an offer to be your wife?"

"I still haven't decided." The words were weighted as he held her away from him, as though he did not trust any further contact. He remained there for a moment longer, perfectly still, every muscle of his body rigid with tension before he stood. He moved for the door.

Elizabeth found herself holding her breath as she listened to his footsteps in the hall, heading farther and farther from her. When his steps faded to nothingness she cradled her head in her hands. What was wrong with her? The man she loved had finally kissed her, and kissed her like he'd enjoyed it very much.

Why did she have to want more?

A few moments later the girls surrounded Elizabeth, exclaiming over her injuries. She assured them she was well and encouraged them to continue with what they'd planned for the afternoon by decorating the hall.

The girls busied themselves, distributing the greens throughout the room, over the door lintels, and along the center of the wide wooden tables.

"Don't you want to help?" Iris asked Elizabeth as she decorated above the hearth with sprigs of holly and ivy.

"You're doing such a wonderful job," Elizabeth replied. "My head hurts me a little, so I'll enjoy watching you." It wasn't a total falsehood. Her head did hurt. The truth, however, was that she wasn't in the least enthusiastic about watching the girls transform the great hall into a holiday setting. Every moment she stayed in the room with them, her unease increased. What if Lucius sent her away?

She obviously wanted more than he was prepared to give her. Finally, she could take sitting quietly with her own thoughts no longer and made her apologies to the girls, then left the chamber and the festivities far behind.

She walked through the manor, her mind and her body reliving Lucius's kiss over and over in a torturous assault. Only two days until their marriage—a marriage that seemed less and less likely to happen. Was she prepared for the consequences if it did not?

Elizabeth shivered as she looked around her. Midwick was a lovely manor. The home she'd always dreamed of having. She gripped the railing and made her way upstairs, and slowly moved down the hallway to the next set of stairs at the end of the hall. The manor's rooms were spacious and airy, with brightly woven tapestries hung on the thick stone walls to block out the chill air so prevalent in Scotland in the wintertime.

She drifted past the three pairs of tall, narrow windows on the upper level. Late-afternoon light filtered through the glass, casting a golden glow at her feet. Drawn by the light, Elizabeth paused by one of the windows and stared wistfully at the landscape covered in snow, which seemed to go on forever. Lucius belonged here. He had always belonged here.

As if summoned by her thoughts, Lucius walked into her line of vision in the courtyard below, leading a large black horse. He was dressed in a tartan of red, blue, and green instead of in his earlier breeches and tunic. The Carrick plaid. With a fluid leap, the kilt-clad Scottish laird tossed himself onto the horse and rode from the courtyard alone.

Elizabeth turned away from the window. She'd driven him away again. With suddenly chilled fingers, she reached up and pulled the linen strip from her head. The bleeding had stopped, as had her dizziness. Perhaps she should leave the manor and forge out on her own while she had a chance to escape with a shred of her dignity intact.

As soon as the thought materialized, she tossed it away. She could never leave without saying good-bye. She knew what it felt like to be left behind with no explanation. She would not treat Lucius or his sisters that way.

She forced her mind away from the laird of the manor and back to the lovely architecture of Midwick. The end of the hallway drew Elizabeth's attention. She had never been up that staircase before. Pulled forward by her own curiosity, she mounted the stairs. At the top, she found herself in yet another hallway, with many doors on each side. Some were open, some closed, yet all the rooms looked as though they'd lain unused for decades.

A shaft of sunlight drew Elizabeth's attention to a place halfway down the hall. At the closed doorway she paused with her hand on the latch, suddenly suffering an odd premonition that she would be better off to leave this room alone. Yet her curiosity won over as she ignored the warning and pushed the latch down.

A musty scent assaulted her as she took her first step inside. A single window cast a bright splash of light into the center of the room, yet left the rest of the chamber in hazy shadow. Elizabeth took another step forward, then another, passing by furnishings that were covered with linen as well as cobwebs and dust.

Grime dimmed the floor. Sheer, lacy webs surrounded unlit candles in the chandelier above her. Despite their linen coverings, Elizabeth could see that a large bed sat in the center of the room along with several chests and a large wardrobe.

After the initial mustiness of the chamber permeated her senses, Elizabeth also thought she detected the faint scent of cinnamon. Lucius? Could this have once been his chamber before he'd left to join the Templars? Had his family closed the entire wing, waiting to reopen it again once he returned?

The walls of the room were bare of tapestries. The only adornment was hidden behind a linen cloth, just like all the other furnishings.

Elizabeth paused before the cloth. For some reason she needed to see what lay hidden beneath. Gripping the corner of the dust-covered cloth, her heart rate quickened as she pulled the cloth away. Her astonished gaze swept the painting from top to bottom. Unbelievable. Nay, it could not be. "Who did this?" she whispered into the void of silence surrounding her.

She could not tear her gaze from the painting of herself reclining on a padded settee, wearing nothing but a slip of the Carrick tartan that covered her from the rise of her breasts to the tops of her thighs. She should have been offended by such a seductive display. Instead a warmth centered in her core and her breath hitched.

She'd never posed for such a work. Even so, the artist had flattered her. Long dark lashes veiled her large brown eyes, and her long tawny hair cascaded loose about her shoulders. Her expression was alive with humor and mischief.

She looked radiant, and decadent, and beautiful, but for whom?

Chapter Six

In the dim light of the chamber, Elizabeth stepped up to the painting. She had to know who had created the image of her. Had the artist signed the piece? As she drew near, she noted a dark scrawl in the right-hand corner. Holding her breath, she bent close: L.C.

Her heart stumbled in her chest. Why would he do such a thing, and from his memory, unless…? She couldn't finish the thought. Something warmed her inside.

Elizabeth stepped back from the painting with a smile and headed from the room. Since the moment she arrived here, she'd done everything wrong. She'd assumed she had no choice but force the issue of their marriage.

In that moment, a whole new world opened itself to her, a world where she was not destined to be in love with a man who would never love her back. Before she saw the painting she'd had no hope that he cared. But why else would he paint this portrait of her, especially wearing almost nothing at all, unless…?

She found herself going back over it all—over everything that had happened since she arrived. Lucius's words said one thing. His actions said another. The confidence she'd lacked earlier in the day suddenly filled her.

She would fight for a future with the man she loved.

She would stay for two more days and expose whatever demons he'd brought back with him to this place. The only chance they had was for him to realize that a new future awaited him if he'd only allow himself to move past his guilt.

In order for that to happen, she had to take another risk. She was not truly the mistress of Midwick yet, but she had to make a lasting impression on Lucius in the next two days. She had to demonstrate her ability to lead the girls wisely. She would be such a proper mistress to his household and his people, and she would show him just how much she cared.

Empowered by her new commitment, Elizabeth made her way downstairs to find the girls had finished decorating the entire manor, inside and out. Greens hung over every doorway, graced the tops of the furnishings, and lined the tables in the great hall. They'd set a brace of candles on each table around the hall as well. When night fell, the room would look like an enchanted garden.

The hall was alive with conversation. Men in tartans of blue and green gathered at the far end of the room. When Elizabeth entered the chamber, Rose hurried to her side.

"Does it please you?" Rose asked, a bit breathless as her gaze shifted from Elizabeth to the men.

"It's magical," Elizabeth replied, her gaze following Rose's. "Are those MacKinley men?"

Rose's cheeks flushed pink as one of the young men at the edge of the group looked her way. "Aye. Our brother brought them here to Midwick to protect us. Isn't it grand?"

"Protect us from whom?" Elizabeth asked with a sudden frown.

"The English. He's worried," she replied with an air of distraction.

Elizabeth chuckled despite the seriousness of the subject Rose had just raised. "And who is the one who can't seem to keep his eyes off you, Rose?"

Another flush of color infused Rose's cheeks as she tore her gaze from the man in question. "Lachlan MacKinley," she whispered.

Elizabeth bit back a smile as she studied the young Scot. His lingering glances at Rose spoke volumes. "Where are the MacKinleys staying?"

"In the stables. Although the stables would be rather dismal in this snow."

Elizabeth's own gaze shifted to the chair she knew Lucius had spent the night in again. "Would they be more comfortable in the house?"

"Oh, aye!"

"Would you and your sisters help me with a task upstairs, then when that's done, help Marie prepare an evening meal for us all?"

"Aye. Lucius must have had a busy morning, because he also brought several of our servants back to us. They are helping Marie in the kitchen right now." The young woman waved for her sisters to join them. "It would be so exciting if we could do something truly special to celebrate our brother's return home."

Elizabeth's cheeks heated as she thought of an altogether different sort of celebration she'd like to have in private with Lucius upon his return. If and when he kissed her again, she would not pull away. "I have an idea," Elizabeth said as the other girls joined her and Rose. "Would you all help me prepare a wedding-Christmastide banquet tomorrow night?"

Five squeals of delight silenced the masculine voices.

Rose's gaze widened. "Did Lucius agree to the marriage?"

Elizabeth forced a stab of doubt away. She could not lose hope. That portrait had to mean something. "Not yet. But he will."

"That's the spirit," Rose said with a smile. "I'm happy to help."

Lily clapped her hands and danced about Elizabeth, her youthful curls bouncing around her shoulders as she did. "Please marry our brother and stay with us forever."

"Having a wedding here would be the very best way to celebrate Christmas Eve." Heather's usually quiet voice was filled with excitement.

"Will there be dancing?" Iris asked with an arched brow.

"I could wear my blue dress." Camellia's gaze shifted to the men. "What a wonderful idea."

"Then let us prepare the celebration." Elizabeth headed toward the stairs with the girls in tow. "Rose, will you see if Marie can spare anyone to help us clean the second-floor rooms? If we work hard, we'll finish just in time to dress for supper."

Rose's smile slipped. She stopped walking, forcing her sisters to do the same. "Lucius asked us never to go up to the second floor."

"Whyever not?"

"I don't think he's ready to face the memories of what our family used to be." She cast a surreptitious glance at Elizabeth. "Peter and Lucius used to rule abovestairs."

Elizabeth brought up her chin. "Sometimes to move forward we have to face the thing that scares us." She offered all the girls a gentle smile. "You let me worry about your brother. Fair enough?"

Each girl nodded in turn.

"I realize I'm asking much of you girls to help with the cleaning, but there isn't the staff to accomplish the task in time."

"We don't mind, Elizabeth. Truly," Rose reassured her.

Heather nodded with a serious expression on her face. "Not if it means having fun later."

Iris frowned. "I hate cleaning, but if you think it will help our brother be more at home with us, I'll help."

"Thank you, Iris, all of you." Elizabeth's gaze passed over all the girls. "Let's think on it as another adventure together."

As Elizabeth climbed each step behind the girls, a sense of joy she hadn't experienced in a long while came over her. She truly would be mistress of Midwick for a while. Whether that was one day or a lifetime, she didn't know. But she was here now and she'd make the most of the opportunity—her first task, to take care of Lucius's chamber and make certain he slept in comfort tonight instead of in that uncomfortable old chair.

❧

By late afternoon, the cleaning was complete. The girls retired to their chambers to prepare for the evening meal. Elizabeth helped each girl coil and pile her hair into an artful arrangement finalized with the additions of ribbons and flowers and jewels in a dress rehearsal for the festivities tomorrow night.

When the girls were satisfied with their appearance, Elizabeth retreated to her chamber to style her own hair. She decided to leave it loose about her shoulders. She held it back on one side with a simple ivory comb.

At the wardrobe, she frowned at her choices. She'd save her best green dress for tomorrow night, but that left only the steel gray broadcloth or the brown linen. She decided on the gray with its simple lines. Smoothing the dress into place against her waist and hips, she accented it with the one piece of jewelry she still possessed of her mother's, a simple silver girdle. She fastened it around her hips with a hint of regret that her father had sold everything else. He'd needed everything and anything saleable to pay off their debts.

Shaking off the past, she palmed the gift she had for Lucius tonight and left the chamber. As she walked toward the steps leading downstairs, she wondered if the new earl had returned home yet.

The thought of seeing him again made her pulse race with both excitement and nervousness, given the way they'd parted last. She started down the hallway and entered the great hall to see the girls were already there and were clustered about the MacKinley men, talking and laughing. Rose was at Lachlan's side. At the sight of

Elizabeth, Rose lifted her hand in a beckoning wave.

Elizabeth nodded and smiled. The smile hitched on her lips a moment later when her gaze locked with Lucius's. He stood with a group of men near the hearth. He was staring at her. She could feel his bold gaze sweep from the top of her tawny hair, over her breasts and hips, right down to her slippered feet, before lifting to her face. Admiration shone in his eyes. He said something to the man beside him and moved away, toward her.

Somehow Elizabeth managed to keep her expression serene, but her treacherous pulse thrummed at her temples at his approach. "Good evening, my lord."

"What gave you the idea that you could authorize a banquet tomorrow night without my consent?"

She couldn't read the expression on his face and for a moment it was difficult to breathe. Was he angry with her for continuing to plan their wedding feast or was he teasing her? She couldn't tell. She wanted to explain herself, but he was watching her so closely she couldn't think clearly. She looked away. "I did it for the girls." She shook her head. "That's a lie. I did it for you."

"I know." He touched her chin, tilted her face, and forced her to meet his gaze. "How is your head?"

"Better, thank you." He looked every inch the gentleman tonight. His claret tunic and dark breeches set off his broad shoulders and his long muscular legs. His dark hair was pulled back at the nape with a thin leather tie.

"Lucius, about that kiss…"

He brought his finger to her lips, stalling any further

words. "For tonight, let's just enjoy each other's company the way we used to. All right?"

She nodded, then smiled. "You're not truly angry about the banquet, are you?"

He returned her smile. "Once again, you made the right decision. It's Christmastide tomorrow, and it's the perfect way to celebrate." He dropped his hand from her chin and his gaze moved past her to those assembled in his hall. "You and the girls have been busy."

"More than you know." She smiled sweetly.

"You always did know how to pique my interest." He looked at her once more. "But I shall ruin your attempt to intrigue me by not asking you anything more."

"You wound me, my lord."

"I'll make it up to you by being your escort to supper."

She felt a small bit of satisfaction that he'd invited her as though she had the option to say no. "I'd be honored." Together they headed for the dais on the opposite side of the chamber. He seated her first before sliding onto the chair beside her. Once they were seated, the other guests followed them to the table.

Rose and Lachlan sat next to each other. "Rose has certainly taken an interest in Lachlan MacKinley," Elizabeth said, nodding in the direction of the young couple.

Lucius's expression darkened. "She's too young to be entertaining thoughts of that kind."

Elizabeth leaned close to him. "They are older than we were when we first—" Kissed. She broke off her words at his dark frown.

"I haven't adjusted to the fact that the girls have matured while I've been away," he said with a frown. His frown remained in place as the meal progressed, making Elizabeth question whether to proceed with her plans. She clutched the small token all the harder as a reminder he was worth the risk. With luck, the keepsake of their past would soften his mood.

By the time the meal ended, her nerves were taut with anticipation. He moved his chair back as though preparing to leave. Her heart leaped. "Lucius?"

He paused and searched her face.

"Before you go…" She reached for his hand, clutching it with her own, passing the item from her warmed palm to his. She pulled her hand away and waited, hardly daring to breathe.

His gaze remained expressionless as he opened his palm and stared at the rock she'd placed there. "You kept this?" He brought his thumb down to caress the surface where years ago he'd scratched You win. L.C. after she'd bested him in one of their many footraces along the length of the loch.

"I treasured it," she said softly.

Any darkness in his face vanished and his lips pulled up into a half smile. "You were so quick footed then."

"Want to see if I still am?" she teased.

His eyes brightened. He flattened his fingers over the rock. "What about the snow?"

"Too much of a challenge for you?"

His grin became devilish. "I never could resist a challenge, especially from you." He took her hand and started from the room. Then he stopped, his gaze moving to Rose and Lachlan. "Perhaps I should stay."

"They are well supervised by Marie and Hadwell, as well as all the other MacKinleys."

Still he hesitated. "I remember my own thoughts about girls at that age," he confessed. "But you're right. They're safe enough here in the great hall if we're only gone a short time." He started forward until they were in the hallway. Grabbing two cloaks from the pegs by the door, he tossed one around her shoulders before he donned the other. "You may regret this," he said, his earlier good humor in place once more as they headed for the loch.

Light from the full moon reflected off what remained of the melting snow, illuminating the night with a silver sheen. The sound of Elizabeth's excited laughter warmed Lucius to his core despite the chill air stinging his face and neck. Elizabeth hurried down the cleared path from the manor to the loch's edge and took up her position. For a moment, he saw the girl she'd been so many years ago—her muddied hem, her hair pulled back, her face alight with laughter. That image vanished and he paused to appreciate the reality before him.

She was still spirited, but as she hitched up the edges of her gown to reveal her stockings and soft leather slippers he realized she'd become a very desirable woman. A woman who could be his wife if he only let go of the past.

He forced his thoughts aside and joined her. "I'll have the advantage over you with my boots, you know."

"The ground is clear of the snow nearest the loch, and

I've been known to run far and fast in these slippers. You're trying to divert my attention. Will you never learn?" she teased.

"Ready?" he asked with a laugh. "To the end of the loch."

She nodded. "One. Two. Three."

On the count, Elizabeth flew across the snow. He ran beside her. She made running appear so effortless. She always could run faster than he could on a sprint, but he could take her every time when they ran for distance. The perfection of the moment washed over him. They'd fallen back into the past so easily tonight: the teasing, the memories, the warmth flowing through him, having her by his side. Joy filled him as he chased after her. No one had ever been able to lighten the darkness inside him as Elizabeth had. She made him feel as light as air, as carefree as a boy, as innocent as the first kiss they'd shared that one warm summer night by the loch.

The thudding rhythm of his heart filled his ears as another more fearful sensation gripped him, consumed him. His footsteps slowed. She surged ahead.

He didn't deserve such joy, and he certainly didn't deserve his old life back. He'd hurt too many people. He stumbled, then stopped.

Her footsteps slowed, then headed back toward him. "Lucius?"

He heard the concern in her voice and turned his back to her. "I can't do this, Elizabeth."

"Race?"

"Nay. I can't give in to my feelings for you." The words

sounded loud in the sudden silence of the night. He drew a sharp breath, trying to control the surge of guilt welling in his chest. He felt so out of place, like a ghost moving through the shadows of his own life. Where he didn't deserve to love or be loved in return.

Elizabeth put her hand on his arm and turned him to face her. "We can take this slowly." He looked at the pallor in her cheeks, the haunted darkness in her brown eyes. "Don't you see you deserve to have joy in your life, especially after everything you've been through?"

His mouth went dry. His palms grew damp, and his guilt grew with each inward breath.

"Talk to me," she whispered.

His gaze skittered away to fix on a clump of snow in the distance. The weight of that guilt became a great, crushing pain in his chest. "I've done so many things wrong," he said brokenly. "Things I can never make right."

"We all have, Lucius. You need to put the past behind you and move forward with your life."

"There are too many reminders," he whispered. "Everywhere I go on the estate, everything I see, reminds me of my father, of Marcus, and how I forsook my duty to them both. Then there's Peter." He swallowed roughly. "He was burned to his death because of my choices. If I'd never joined the Templars, he never would have followed me. He'd be alive today if only…"

"Lucius, don't torture yourself over things you cannot change. You cannot deny your father, Marcus, even Peter their own choices, their own lives. They were not your puppets, but grown men with destinies of their own."

He said nothing, simply letting the night and the darkness engulf him.

"Your brothers are gone," she continued. "Your sisters, however, are very much alive and in need of their brother. You said that's why you came home. You wanted to spare them the penury that would befall them if your uncle assumed the estate and the title."

She stared at him, challenged him. "Rose is eighteen. She deserves the chance with Lachlan to see if they can make a match. Camellia, Heather, Iris, and eventually Lily all deserve that as well. They deserve a chance to make their place in this world. Then if after they are settled, you choose to leave it all behind, that's your choice."

He clenched his jaw against the reminder of his duty. "And what of my duty to you?"

She flinched. "It is I who owe you, my lord. Not the other way around. Your family paid my father's debts as a part of our betrothal contract. You own me every bit as much as you own the estate and all it entails."

He owned her. He wanted her. But could he take on that responsibility without crushing her as he had the others he'd loved? Lucius clutched his fists at his sides, fighting the urge to pull her close. He wanted to wrap himself in her warmth and maybe, just maybe, feel like he didn't deserve to be alone.

But he was afraid.

She looked at him, and in the depths of her eyes he saw the pain he'd caused, and something else, something he couldn't name. She kept staring at him, saying nothing. Silence stretched between them, one that began to nibble at his confidence in his decision. "Don't look at me that way."

"What way?"

"As if you know I'll change my mind."

"You will." Her voice trembled just a bit, belying the conviction of her words. Then softer, she said, "We belong together."

Chapter Seven

Did he hear what he thought he heard? For a moment he felt a flash of pure hope before his usual guilt swamped him. Did he truly deserve the joy she spoke of earlier?

"I know you have feelings for me, whether you choose to express them or not," Elizabeth said softly.

"Have I said—?"

"I saw the painting."

She'd seen the painting? His breath stilled in his chest as embarrassment warred with confusion. "Now you know my deepest secrets."

"Nay," she said softly. "Your secrets are still your own. I have no idea why you painted me or what the portrait truly means. Perhaps you'll explain it to me in time."

He wanted to accuse her of overstepping her bounds, wanted to make her feel as exposed as he felt right now. "You had no right to go upstairs and into my old chamber. The girls know better."

He was glad when she flinched. "They went to the second floor because I asked them. They only wanted to please you, as did I." She drew back from him. "What I found in your bedchamber was much more than I expected. And I'm not talking about the painting. You've abandoned that room and that part of your life. Why?"

He frowned. "It was easier to abandon my past than

revisit it."

She met his gaze. "The past and our experiences there can be a teacher instead of a tormentor. Sometimes we have to go through certain trials in order to become the person we are today." Elizabeth's gaze sharpened on him. "Perhaps it's time you to face your demons, Lucius. Then, maybe you'll find the happiness you are withholding from yourself."

She turned and strode away from him, heading back to the manor, leaving him alone in the chill night as the truth of her words resonated within him.

Was she right? Was he prolonging his own suffering by not accepting his past?

After the house had settled for the night, Lucius crept up the two flights of stairs to his old room. He stood in front of the partially open door. He clutched a brace of candles in his hand as grief rippled through him, one wave after another, leaving him chilled and unsettled.

He couldn't seem to make himself move forward into the chamber. He just stood there, seeing a hundred moments pass through his mind's eye. Like the time he'd won his first mock battle against Marcus…or the day Peter had been thrown from his horse and broken his collarbone…their first hunting trip together…the day he'd kissed Elizabeth…Peter's thirteenth birthday…Marcus's laughter as they told each other stories late into the night…

He forced the memories away, refusing to let them keep

him trapped forever. He had to stop pretending and face whatever reality lay before him. He thrust the door wide and stepped inside. The golden glow from the candles seeped into the shadows.

His heartbeat thundered in his ears as he stepped further into the chamber and slowly, numbly, moved about his room, touching anything and everything in his path—the table near the bedside with the small wooden cross he kept there, a silver bowl holding a dried rabbit's foot, a shark's tooth, and three Roman coins Peter had collected and given to him as gifts over the years.

He moved to the bed and brushed the clean woolen tartan cloth covering the ticking beneath. At the window he traced his fingers over the chilled pane. It was so rare to have anything but shutters in homes such as theirs. But his father had insisted on the expensive luxury and had sent four of his men to Vienna by ship to bring a dozen leaded panes home.

For a moment, his grief swelled. It had been five years ago his father died. He missed his father, but he'd learned to live without him during the time he'd been away. He smoothed his fingers over the glass once more before turning away.

Finally, when he could no longer avoid looking at her image, Lucius brought his gaze to the portrait he'd painted of Elizabeth. His mother had insisted he learn to paint with an instructor when she'd discovered his novice attempts kept hidden in the cellar. He'd used boiled berries and bark mixed with egg whites to create his paints.

He'd painted the portrait the night after he'd found

Elizabeth and Marcus kissing in the garden. "God's blood, Marcus. Why did you have to intrude where you didn't belong?"

But it wasn't the kiss that weighed him down. It was the neglect he'd assumed toward his family. Lucius shifted his gaze to the wood-beam ceiling overhead and clenched his jaw against the familiar pain. He couldn't continue this wretched cycle of sadness, grief, and guilt. He had to pull himself out of it.

What he needed were new memories of this place and the people he loved who were still very much present in his life. He drew a steadying breath. Resolved to move forward, he grabbed the brace of candles from his bedside table and headed for the door, to the one person who could help him.

Elizabeth.

Silently he crept down the stairs and to the chamber where she slept. At her door, he knocked softly. No response. He tried the latch. The door opened soundlessly and he stepped into the room.

A wedge of yellow-bright light penetrated the darkness of her chamber as he made his way to her bedside. She slept with the blankets entwined around her slender curves. At the sight of her, his body ached. Desire that had lain dormant through his years as a warrior flared to life.

"Elizabeth?" he whispered.

She startled awake. "Lucius?" She shifted the blankets to cover her body. "What are you doing here?" Her voice was smooth and husky with sleep.

"I came to ask a favor of you."

She sat up and pulled her woolen chemise up on her shoulders. "Go on," she encouraged.

He didn't really know what to say. He hadn't known since the moment she walked back into his life two days ago. And yet he'd never felt more alive than he did right now. He drew in the scent of her. "Will you go with me to the outcropping where we used to play?"

"Now?"

He nodded. "You said I needed to make new memories. I want to watch the sun rise over the grassland with you."

Her gaze narrowed on him. "Can't sleep?"

He nodded.

She swung her legs over the edge of the bed. "I'll need to dress. What if I meet you downstairs in a few moments?"

He smiled. "Thank you," he said as he set the candleholder near her bedside and removed one of the two candles. He left the room, softly shutting the door behind him. A sense of lightness came to him as he made his way downstairs to wait.

It didn't take long to saddle a horse, and riding double, they emerged into the night, heading north, away from the manor. He guided the horse toward the outcropping in the distance and looked up at the stars twinkling in the clear night sky. A soft wind crept past them and the leafless trees sparkled with their coating of frost and ice. Beneath the horse's feet, the snow had started to melt, leaving barren patches here and there across the landscape.

"I'd forgotten how beautiful the scenery is here," Lucius said.

"I imagine you've seen many wonderful things in the past few years," she replied.

He tried to recall anything that rivaled this moment and could think of none. "It's interesting how beautiful home looks when you've been away for a while."

"I'm certain that's true," she said softly.

When they arrived at the outcropping, Lucius dismounted, then offered Elizabeth his hand. "I know you're more than capable of getting off this horse yourself, but indulge me."

"Isn't that why we are here in the middle of the night?"

He chuckled and helped her down. As she slid down beside him, her cloak opened and he could feel her warmth against him. And again he hungered to feel her lying in his arms, her body entwined with his the way her bedsheets had wrapped her earlier.

His body clenched at the reminder she was his by the terms of their betrothal agreement to do with as he pleased. The knowledge was a potent elixir against his will. He couldn't pull his gaze from the temptation of her mouth. It was all he could do not to pull her into his arms and taste her lips. They were as dark and inviting as he remembered.

"Shall we climb to the top?" she asked, breaking into his thoughts, making him more aware of the enchantment she held him in. She withdrew two steps, but not before he noted the color in her cheeks. Even in the moonlight there was no mistaking she'd been as affected by his nearness as he was by hers.

He tied the horse's reins loosely about a nearby bush, all the while trying to force the memory of her warmth and softness from his thoughts. They were here to build memories of a different kind.

He tossed the saddlebag over his shoulder and hesitated at the sight of Elizabeth. Her hair fell free around her shoulders to her waist, wavy from the earlier braid she'd worn. Beneath the silver moonlight, she was as much the tempting siren as he'd painted her to be.

Since the moment she returned to his life, he'd been assailed by old feelings and emotions. Part of him wanted to hold her and kiss her, while the other part wanted to run as he had before, as far away from her, as fast as he could.

But he'd tried running away once, and it hadn't banished her from his thoughts. He released a heartfelt sigh. Did that mean he should hold her and kiss her instead? Was that the new memory he wanted to make here this night?

Lucius's emotions warred inside him. His intention had been merely to spend time with her—to create new memories—and yet the sight of her wild innocence, her sweet scent, the feel of her warmth were almost more than he could bear. He craved her on a level he did not understand. She filled him with more than just lust; she did things to him he'd never been able to comprehend.

"Lucius?" she asked, with sudden curiosity lighting her wide, brown eyes.

"Let's go." He reached for her hand, and together they hiked the short distance up the rocky ledge to sit atop a huge outcropping of slate.

At the top she smiled. "I remember being here as children and thinking this was the farthest I'd ever seen."

"When it's clear, you can see all the way to England from here." He cleared the ledge of the remaining snow before he set the saddlebag down and gathered wood into the center of the rock.

It wasn't long before cheery flames glowed and sparks fluttered above the fire. The crackling of the wood as it burned peppered the darkness with noise. The warmth of the bonfire pressed back the chill of the night enough so that Lucius had removed his cloak and set it on the rock beneath them.

Elizabeth sat a ways from him and reclined on her elbows against the soft fur that lined his cloak. She stared at the star-filled sky, looking as content before the fire's heat as a feline. At the sight of her, a different sort of need he hadn't felt in years suddenly consumed him. He reached for his saddlebag and withdrew a sheaf of linen and a charcoal he'd tossed inside. He spread the paper on the rock beside him. The faint scratching noise of his charcoal filled the silence.

"What are you doing?" Elizabeth asked, turning to face him.

"Come see for yourself."

She hesitated for a moment before she stood and moved cautiously to his side. "You can't be drawing the view, because we can't see any—" She gasped and unsteadily sank to her knees beside him. "You're drawing me."

He kept his gaze fixed on the drawing, unable to see what emotion her eyes might reveal. He'd drawn her as he'd seen her by the fire. Even in only shades of black and grey he'd managed to capture the fire in her gaze, the high color in her cheek, the wild disarray of her hair.

This was not the woman he remembered from the past. She was an entirely different woman from the one he'd left five years ago.

Chapter Eight

Elizabeth stared in wonder at the drawing Lucius had created of her. The image he'd drawn was far more sensual than the painting in his chamber, although this time all her clothes were on. It was the look in her eyes that said it all.

Her breath hitched. "Lucius…" His name fell from her lips in a breathless whisper of longing.

His fingers stalled a hairbreadth above the linen. "Do you approve?"

"Aye." Their gazes met and she was enthralled by the possibilities she saw there. She knew then, as certainly as she'd ever known anything in her life, something had changed. He was no longer the young man who'd run away five years ago. The pain and regret that had been ever present in his eyes since his return was gone.

He was close enough that she could feel the silken rush of his breath against her cheek. If she leaned forward she could bring her lips into contact with his. And if she did, this time she wouldn't have the power within herself to pull away. Instead of leaning forward she found herself saying, "How do you create such details?"

He shrugged. "Images linger in my mind."

His words, however innocent, revealed so much. No wonder he had such a difficult time letting go of his memories. They were etched on his mind in a different fashion than for most people. "You should paint more," she said quietly.

"Come sit by me." He patted the empty space on the woolen cloak beside him and set his drawing aside. "We must speak."

Elizabeth's heart faltered. Was she wrong in thinking she'd seen something different in his gaze only moments before? Was that what this outing was all about, one last moment together before they would part forever?

He moved to face her. "What do you want from this arrangement between our families?"

"I want to honor the betrothal that has been negotiated. I want to save my father's reputation."

He turned to face her. "Nay, Elizabeth. That's what your father wants you to say." He frowned. "What do you want?"

She stared up at him, startled. What did she want? Could he not see that in her eyes? He was the man she'd always dreamed of. She wanted him to love her, dance with her, and laugh with her, and hold her late into the night, to embrace their children, for the two of them to grow old together. But how could she say that to him?

He reached for her hand. "Answer me, Elizabeth."

"I want you as my husband."

Before she could go on, he captured her lips, and she moaned at the taste of him. He tasted like all the things she wanted in this life and had never attained. She wanted him, she'd always wanted him, despite her engagement to another man.

A catch came to her breath as Lucius reclined into her, easing her back against the fur-lined cloak. His free hand brushed over her back and he deepened his kiss. His hand on her back delved lower, to cup her bottom and press her hips closer to his. She felt the swell of his manhood as he rocked against her.

Sensations flowed through her as every fiber of her being quivered, came alive. She curled her hand around the nape of his neck and anchored him to her. Her eyes fastened on his and something deep in her soul expanded. I am his. No matter what happened after tonight. In this moment they belonged together as one.

She knew nothing about joining with a man, but she hoped instinct would guide the way. As if sensing her capitulation, Lucius eased her back against his cloak and unfastened the hook on hers. He set her cloak aside and slowly his fingers slipped behind her to release the ribbons of her gown. A heartbeat later he unfastened her gown and sent it sliding over her head. Her chemise followed, leaving her naked. The warmth of the fire reached around her, banishing the chill.

He pulled back from her and removed his boots, his scabbard, then his tunic and breeches, until he lay naked beside her once more, his manhood boldly erect. How beautiful he was.

He gathered her discarded cloak and pulled it over their bodies, shielding them from the cold. In the warmth of the cocoon he'd created, he took her hand and placed her palm against his chest. She could feel the thunder of his heartbeat vibrating through his body and into her own through her palm. Emboldened by the knowledge he was as aroused as she, Elizabeth smoothed her hand down the planes of his chest. She could feel his muscles bunch and release beneath her touch. She delighted in her power over him as she explored the smooth warm flesh over supple muscles and traced the line of dark, wiry hair to where it encircled his manhood.

"You must cease doing that," he said, the sound guttural. Before she could touch him there, he lifted her palm to his lips and placed a tender kiss against her flesh. "I want us to take our time. If you touch me there, I'll be lost."

Before she could ask him to explain, he trailed his fingers over her body, and everywhere he touched was blessed with fire—her breasts, her throat, her belly, her thighs. His hands nudged her legs apart and he moved between them. His head bent and he slowly rubbed his cheek back and forth on her belly. The faint abrasion of his stubble against her bare flesh was wildly exciting.

His teeth nipped gently at her flesh, then his tongue followed to soothe and tease. She could feel his warm breath on her flesh, and the muscles of her belly tightened in response. Every muscle vibrated at an excruciating pitch of anticipation.

He brought his head up and smiled at her, and Elizabeth caught her breath. This is how he should look all the time. Relaxed, with his face alight with laughter and joy. He would have looked that way had the humor not been stolen from him by years of isolation and grief.

She wanted to give him back those years he'd lost, give

him back his joy, with a desire springing as much from protectiveness as it did from passion. Her hand moved up to cup his cheek, then smooth back the hair from the side of his face. "I shall remember this moment always, Lucius."

"Me too," he said, his voice thick. His finger delved between her thighs, searching the inner warmth of her womanhood. He found the nub for which he searched and began to slowly rotate with his finger.

She cried out as a searing jolt of need streaked through her.

His gaze was warm with pleasure as he watched her face. "Does this please you?"

She curled her fingers in his hair. "Aye." She could scarcely breathe through the glorious haze of pleasure he created inside her.

"Good." Two fingers plunged inside.

She cried out into the night air as the intensity of his stroke increased, creating both pleasure and hunger. "Lucius, please."

He bent his head and claimed her lips, silencing her plea. His fingers left her as he positioned himself over her and slid within her, slowly, letting her become accustomed to him, to his fullness. When he met with resistance, he paused.

"I'm sorry for this," he said. He tensed before he thrust forward.

She cried out as pain spasmed through her, then just as suddenly faded away until she was again aware of only the sensations of fullness, of pleasure.

He began to move, alternating short strokes with long ones, depth with shallowness, swiftness with long, leisurely slowness.

Elizabeth caressed his back and realized as she did that small scars zigzagged across his left shoulder to his right side. Had a sword inflicted the wound? Her heart clenched. He'd suffered so much pain.

Slowly, lovingly, she trailed her fingers up and down the scar. She wanted him to know by her touch that regardless, she found him perfect in every way. The scent and feel of him washed over her.

Love me, Lucius.

The words were a prayer deep in her soul. He was all she'd ever wanted in this life. He had always been the symbol of everything good to her. He was love. Honor. Passion.

And as though he'd heard her prayer, he plunged deep, filling her until it was as though they were one. His palms cupped her bottom, lifting her to each thrust until the glory of the moment released in a rapture that shook her to the depths of her soul. She heard Lucius's cry above her as the same wonder claimed him.

They hung there, in that moment of bliss, where nothing and no one mattered except the delicious enjoyment they'd given each other. Their hearts beat as one. Their breathing mingled until slowly the moment faded and reality returned.

The crisp air enveloped their cocoon of warmth as he slipped beside her and laid his head against her shoulder. She could feel the vibration of his heart against her own.

She reached up and toyed with the ends of his hair as she cradled his body with her own.

Neither of them spoke in the quietness of the night. Lucius grasped the cloak that she'd worn and pulled it over the two of them. She kissed his brow. "Sleep for a while," she breathed.

"The sunrise." His words were light and airy and already sleepy.

"We'll know when it's time." She tightened her arms around him, praying for many more times like this to share with the man she loved. Closing her eyes, she held tight to that hope.

Lucius's eyes opened at the sound of a rooster crowing in the distance. The sound vibrated through the chilled predawn air. He reached down in the semidarkness and tugged the woolen cloak up tighter against Elizabeth's chin, then took a deep, satisfying breath of the morning air.

He stretched one arm, then the other. Every muscle in his body shrieked in protest at the movement. He continued to stretch, reveling in the stiffness of his legs and torso, and grinned. He'd earned this pain, not by sleeping in a chair near the hearth, but because he'd slept on a rock alongside the most desirable woman in the world.

Praise the saints, it felt good!

"Elizabeth," he whispered as he stroked her cheek, allowing his fingers to tangle in her hair as they had last night. "The sunrise."

She groaned and her eyes flickered open. "Did we miss it?"

His smile increased at her disheveled state. She looked as though she'd been thoroughly pleasured. At the thought, his body hardened, wanting to explore her hidden secrets once more.

The sky turned a pale orangish pink as she sat up. He slipped his arm around her shoulders and drew her close, and was pleased when she leaned against his shoulder. Her being near him seemed like the most natural thing in the world.

"Elizabeth," he said softly, trying to find a way to say what was in his heart. In this moment with her, he felt his grief lessen and something new, more hopeful, take a grip on his soul.

She turned her face up to his and remained silent, though the warmth in her eyes gave him the courage to go on.

"I'm sorry for how I treated you when you arrived at Midwick. I was afraid to…" He paused, knowing once he said the words he could never take them back. "I was afraid to care about anyone the way I cared about you."

She smiled up at him. "I understand you were afraid I'd break your heart again."

He felt the corner of his mouth quirk into a smile as he turned quickly away, staring once again at the slight blossom of orange creeping up from the horizon. "I still have a ways to go to put the past behind me."

"Everything doesn't have to happen overnight. We have

time, Lucius."

He flashed her a grin. "Aye, we have time." Off in the distance, the sun was coloring the horizon a fiery red. Yet the woman beside him drew his interest far more, and he brought down his head and touched his mouth to hers. He brushed his lips across the softness of hers, and she gave a small gasp. Her taste flowed into him, a familiar honey. A lifetime of wanting clutched his chest, his gut, and he deepened the kiss. He brought his hand to rest against the small of her back, pulling her closer.

The kiss seemed to go on forever, with neither of them pulling away until a glint of sunlight caressed his closed eyelids, urging him to focus his attention on the reason for this outing. With a groan of remorse he broke the kiss. "Sunrise," he whispered.

She pressed her cheek against his chest and looked into the distance with a soft gasp.

His gaze shifted from her to the horizon, and what he saw made his breath catch in his throat. It wasn't the cloudless vibrant sky that seemed to start at his toes and reach up endlessly to the heavens above. It wasn't the realization that nothing stood between him and his God except that rising sun.

It was the flecks of surging brown and gray against a background of white snow that stole the breath from his lungs. Lucius shot to his feet, startling Elizabeth.

"The English are invading."

Chapter Nine

Lucius grabbed his boots and slammed his feet into them. "Elizabeth, we must hurry and alert the others."

"The girls," Elizabeth whispered.

Lucius's heart clenched. "We'll reach them in time." They dressed in silence. Once they were done, he took her hand, and together they flew down the outcropping to the horse.

The MacKinleys were gathered in the hall breaking their fast when Lucius threw the door open with a bang and charged into the suddenly silent room. "The English are attacking!"

The words had the desired effect, as the MacKinleys surged to life and reached for their weapons.

"We should send a rider tae alert the clans." Malcolm MacKinley strapped his sword at his hips and grasped his battle-ax.

Lucius nodded. "Send one of your men to ride for the clans. I want everyone prepared for that raiding party this time."

Jacob Insley had entered the great hall and joined the men. "The Insleys will assist ye. We're nae many, but those of us who are here will fight the English at yer side. I'll assemble the men."

Lucius nodded. "My thanks, Jacob."

Elizabeth drew closer. "What can I do? There must be something."

Lucius schooled his features to remain blank. He had to hide from Elizabeth the uncertainty he felt. "Go to the girls. Ask Rose to show you where the hidden chamber is in the cellar. All of you stay inside. No matter what happens. You are safer there than anywhere else."

At her nod, he leaned forward and kissed her on the lips. "For luck," he said a heartbeat before he left her there.

They would need all the luck they could get to push back the English with so few men.

The morning light glinted off the mist that lingered in pockets above the melting snow as the English marched in a column across the open grasslands.

Lucius gripped his sword in one hand, his dagger in the other. The English had forty men to the Scots' twenty. He forced his mind to clear and tensed for battle. His horse settled, waiting for the command that would launch them forward. Out of the edges of his vision, Lucius could see the MacKinleys and the Insleys prepare themselves for the mounted charge. Amos, Silas, Malcolm, Jacob, Lachlan, and his other clansmen perched behind him, waiting for his command. Every man he could see was focused on the battle ahead.

Lucius moved the men silently forward. At their approach, one of the Englishmen at the front of the column stiffened like a hound catching the scent of fresh blood. The man twisted toward them. He jerked on the reins of his horse and called an abrupt halt to the forward motion of the column. The man's eyes narrowed. He donned his helmet. A shrill call shattered the sudden silence.

In response, Lucius's throat vibrated with the roar of a battle cry as old and savage as his Scottish ancestry. His kin flung themselves forward to meet their enemies head-on. The men in the first charge brought their targes up and, with the screech of metal against metal, warded off the first strike of the enemy's swords.

The clansmen continued forward, dispatching the enemy, breaking their line as they forced their way up the center of the column. Lucius charged, engaging another horseman in an explosive clash of swords. He deflected the blow, then pulled his dagger free and thrust up into the horseman's side. The body fell. He pulled his weapon free as all around him, his kin wielded lethal blows, sending the English to the ground moaning their defeat as the Scots crippled their offenses.

The acrid taste and smell of war burned Lucius's lungs as he charged forward again. Shouts of the enemy clashed with the roar of the clans. Men on both sides fell from their horses to battle on foot.

A roar sounded behind him. Lucius maneuvered his horse, twisting around just in time to slash open the chest of an Englishman who bore down on Malcolm, fighting on horseback at his side.

" 'Tis thankful I am that the Templars taught ye how tae fight," Malcolm said before he engaged a new foe.

Lucius could only grunt in response as another

horseman bore down on him.

"I'll have your head!" cried the Englishman, who appeared to be the leader.

Lucius ducked as the man's blade hacked down in an arc across his shoulders. The motion set Lucius off balance and he tumbled from his horse. Lucius threw himself against the earth and came up instantly with his sword at the ready. Two men rushed forward on foot. The first man battered Lucius's broadsword to cut away his defense. But Lucius managed to block each blow as he palmed his dagger and thrust it through the air into one man's chest. The second man charged. Lucius drew a breath and prepared for the impact of sword against sword. The screech and clangor of steel filled the air, as did the noisy inhalations and exhalations as their weapons came together.

Lucius waited for an opening. Seeing it, he slashed the man's arm. His opponent groaned and dropped his weapon a heartbeat before Lucius sent him to his grave. All around him, his kin did the same. They fought with skill and courage, despite the odds, as the conflict turned in their favor.

Beside him, Amos and Lachlan charged forward as a unit, wielding their axes with proficient skill, carving a path through the enemy as efficiently as though they were chopping down trees.

A roar of rage sounded behind Lucius. He turned just as the leader of these men hurled into him, slamming him to the ground. The man's bulk trapped him momentarily until Lucius brought his knee up to connect with the man's privates.

Roaring obscenities and groaning in pain, the man rolled to the side. Yet another Englishman charged Lucius while he was down, carving a glittering arc through the air with his sword.

Lucius rolled to one side with only a sliver of air to spare as the blade missed his throat and thumped into the soil beneath the snow.

Drawing on all his strength and speed, Lucius leaped up and slashed his new opponent in the front of the legs before forcing his blade down into the chest of the fallen leader, feeling the weapon bite through hard flesh. The man hissed, his gaze connecting with Lucius's.

"He said you'd be an easy conquest." The Englishman grimaced.

"Who?" Lucius demanded. The sounds of the battle din faded for Lucius as he listened to the man's labored breathing.

"All we cared about…was killing Scots and…taking his money."

Lucius dropped to his knees beside the man. "You did this for a few miserable coins?"

The man's lips pulled up in a sly grin. "A thousand groats…ain't miserable. 'Tis good sense."

Someone paid these men to attack. Who and why? Lucius moved closer to hear the man's words over his ragged breathing. The Englishman's hands shot up to grip Lucius's neck, but there was no strength left in his fingers to do more than leave a bloody smear as his hands drooped to the snow-covered ground.

"Who paid you?"

The man's breathing stuttered.

"Tell me," Lucius growled, even though he feared he already knew the answer to his own question. He needed confirmation.

The man's smile went lax. His eyes rolled back and his breathing ceased.

Lucius growled his frustration. The sound of horses and shouts of the English filled the air as the remaining English warriors fled at the sight of their fallen leader.

Lucius stood. He released a harsh breath and wiped his sword on his tunic before sheathing the weapon. The battle was over, but he still couldn't shake the chill that snaked down his spine. A thousand groats.

"Something is amiss," Lucius said as he joined the MacKinleys and the Insleys, who'd already gathered their two injured men from the aftermath of the battle.

Lachlan slipped his ax into the leather sheath on his back and hurried to Lucius's side. "We fared better than I expected," the young man boasted.

"These were not English soldiers. At least not the heavily trained and armored ones we are used to confronting."

Malcolm nodded wearily. "Who were they then?"

"Hired mercenaries, if we are to believe their leader." Lucius frowned. "If only he hadn't died before he could say who hired him."

Silas shrugged. "So they were out for a pre-Christmastide plunder."

"It's more than that. Something much darker is at

play here." Lucius's gaze drifted back in the direction of Midwick Manor. "God's toes—"

"You don't think this was merely a ploy to…?" Lachlan's face mirrored Lucius's dread.

Lucius's heart faltered. "Aye, I do."

Amos MacKinley's heavily bearded face paled. "You think they waited for us to leave, then marched on Midwick Manor?"

Lucius didn't bother answering. He ran to his horse, mounted, and spurred it toward his home. He knew in the depth of his soul that that's exactly what had happened. His heart pounded as fear took root inside him. He couldn't have allowed this to happen again. He'd failed Peter. Marcus. His father. Now his sisters, and… He gave vent to his emotions with an inhuman sound that was part howl and part cry. He had to get back to Elizabeth and his sisters before it was too late.

For the first time since Peter died, Lucius prayed. He breathed every prayer he remembered as he urged his horse to fly over the snowy terrain. Those prayers caught in his throat as he neared the manor and saw the two MacKinleys he'd left to guard the manor while the girls hid tumbled on the ground near the front of the house. Lucius threw back his head and howled in agony and rage. He jumped from his horse before it stopped, and rushed through the open doorway into his home.

He skidded to a halt inside the great hall to find Marie lying facedown in a pool of her own blood near the hearth. Lucius's stomach clenched as he hastened to her side and turned the old woman over. The flesh at her shoulder had been splayed open, yet she still lived.

Marie drew short shallow breaths. Her pale blue eyes flickered open and filled with agony. "My lord. I tried…"

Lucius grabbed a length of linen from the table behind him and pressed it against the woman's wound.

"Rest easy. You're going to be all right. I'll see to that."

She shook her head. "He took them all. I tried to stop him…" Marie choked on a sob. "He knew where they were hidden."

Only a family member would know about the secret chamber belowstairs. "Horatio," Lucius said, trying desperately to keep his fear and his anger in check.

Shuffling footsteps sounded behind Lucius. He drew his sword and turned as he came to his feet. Hadwell staggered through the doorway, his face covered in blood from a severe beating. From his injuries, it was apparent the steward had fought valiantly to try to save the girls from abduction.

"Horatio took the girls," the steward sputtered before he collapsed to his knees.

Behind Hadwell, the MacKinleys raced into the hall. Malcolm and Silas gripped the steward beneath his arms and helped him to his feet.

"Bring Hadwell here and sit him in a chair," Lucius directed as he lifted Marie and placed her in a chair. He signaled Amos MacKinley to join him. "Press this against her wound," he told the man, releasing the linen for Amos to take over. "Silas, heat your dagger in the fire and seal the wound on her shoulder when you can."

"The other servants?" Lucius asked. "Where are they?"

"Some fled to the safety of the village. Others are hiding in the chambers abovestairs," Hadwell said, then winced with pain.

"Jayne and the children?" Lucius asked with his heart in his throat.

Jacob Insley hurried into the great hall. At the relief on his face, Lucius drew an easier breath.

"Jayne, Maybel, and the baby are well. They hid in the wardrobe when they heard the commotion."

"Praise the saints," Marie breathed.

"At least there are some blessings in all this chaos." Lucius gave Marie a bittersweet smile.

Her eyes filled with tears. "He left me alive tae tell ye…" Marie said raggedly. "He wants ye tae leave Midwick and return to the Templars. If ye don't, he threatened tae kill the girls."

Silas and Malcolm erupted into curses.

"We have to go after them," Lachlan growled from his location near the chamber door. "I saw wagon tracks in what's left of the snow. We can follow him."

"It's not the girls he wants," Amos MacKinley scoffed. "He wants the estate. He made no secret of that while yer father was alive."

Lachlan gripped his sword. "I'm ready to fight."

"What will ye do, Lord Carrick? Will ye go back tae the Templars and spare the girls?" Silas asked.

"My place is here with my sisters." Lucius's thoughts whirled as he sought a plan. "Marie, was Horatio alone or did he have others with him?"

"He had two men with him when he arrived," she

replied.

"He only left with one," Hadwell replied with a bitter laugh. "Why do ye think I look like this? The man landed a few punches, but I got the best of him. He's tied up in the cellar."

"Good man, Hadwell." Lucius patted the man gently on the shoulder. "Two men with six women could not have traveled far, even if Horatio stole our wagon. The land here is flat and open, with very few places to hide."

"With twenty of us, we can overtake the two men easily."

Hadwell staggered to his feet. "I'd be honored to join ye, my lord."

Lucius gently clasped the old man's shoulder once more with gratitude. "I need you here, Hadwell, to make certain Marie and the others are protected. And when all this is over, you and I and the men will build pele towers to protect our people."

He straightened. "Agreed."

"They can't die," Marie said softly from her place near the hearth.

Panic snaked through Lucius at her words, but he forced the emotion away. "They'll be back before nightfall." Lucius held on to that fraying shred of hope as he headed for his horse. He would find them, his sisters and Elizabeth, and he would make their world right.

Uncle Horatio had unsettled his sisters' lives for the very last time. Lucius had been too weighed down with guilt when he'd returned to see his responsibilities clearly. But that mantle of guilt was gone. The earldom was his and he would wear that responsibility with pride. His sisters needed his protection and his love. And Elizabeth… She deserved so much more than he had given her so far.

Lucius mounted his horse. Lachlan started off on foot, following the trail left in the melting snow by the wagon wheels. At Lucius's signal, his kin headed for the tree-lined area near the loch.

He would find Elizabeth and his sisters. He would bring them home, because if he failed he didn't think he could survive such a loss once again.

Chapter Ten

Faint from cold, without the protection of cloaks or wraps, the girls huddled together in the wagon. Their hands were tied together before them, then tied with a lead from one set of hands to another in a chain: Iris, Camellia, Rose, Lily, Heather, then Elizabeth. Only Iris and Elizabeth were not bound on both sides.

A dark stranger drove the wagon while the girls' Uncle Horatio twisted toward them, his sword drawn and poised to strike. Elizabeth positioned herself closest to the man so that if he decided to use the weapon, it would be she, not the girls, who took the man's violence.

With every step, Elizabeth's heartbeat thudded in her ears. Her mind raced with ways they could escape once the wagon stopped. They were tied together so closely that it made walking difficult and running next to impossible.

Back at the manor they'd been wrestled to the ground and bound by Horatio and his accomplice before the men shoved them into the wagon. The vehicle rolled alongside the western tree-lined edge of the loch, heading south toward the border with England.

Their direction sent a ripple of fear across the nape of Elizabeth's neck, as did the large cask Horatio and the driver had lifted into the back of the wagon. An odd scent came from the cask—a scent Elizabeth couldn't quite place.

Elizabeth returned her gaze to the madman who'd abducted them. He planned to use them as bait either to force Lucius back to the Templars or to lure him to his death.

The second option would never come to pass, not while she still drew breath. But for now, she had to find a way to protect the girls. Elizabeth shifted back against the side of the wagon. If only she could stop the wagon by forcing the wheel to come off, or break. Two men trying to maneuver six women over the English border would have a difficult time.

"Once we clear the loch, which way do we go?" the driver asked Horatio.

When Horatio turned his gaze from her to talk to the man, the sword in his hands dipped.

Elizabeth quickly glanced at Heather, hoping the girl would understand and follow her lead. Elizabeth brought her bound hands up and gripped the flat of the blade between her palms and twisted her arms. The sword jerked out of Horatio's grasp and flew over the side of the wagon.

"God's blood!" Horatio thundered. He lurched forward in his seat, grabbing Elizabeth by the throat.

Elizabeth gasped and clawed at the man's hands. The wagon picked up speed as the driver turned to see what the ruckus was about.

With a terrified shriek, the horse lurched forward, picking up speed as it darted ever closer to the trees at the water's edge.

"Stop that," Horatio bit out.

"Yer upsettin' the horse," the driver yelled.

"Let go of her!" Heather struck her uncle in the head with her bound hands.

Horatio yelped. His grip on Elizabeth relaxed.

Heather struck him again, this time harder, setting him off balance. The wagon lurched again, and Horatio tumbled over the side, followed immediately by a thump and a buck of the wagon as the rear wheel hit his body.

An agonized cry pierced the air.

A creak sounded.

"Hold on to each other," Elizabeth snapped to the girls. Before the words were out, the wheel buckled and the conveyance pitched downward. It hit the ground hard, sending wood splintering as it dug into the earth. At the impact, the cask flew out the back. Camellia grabbed Iris to keep her from being crushed as the girls tumbled over the edge.

The rope burned against Elizabeth's wrists as she rolled to a stop on the ground. "Is everyone unharmed?" she asked, righting herself. She frantically looked over the others, who appeared undamaged.

A terrible scream sounded. The horse shot forward. The terrified animal dodged a tree at the edge of the loch, but the wagon did not. An explosion filled the air. Elizabeth drew a startled breath as wood debris flew back at them. She threw her arms over the girls' heads, trying to protect them.

When silence settled, she shook the debris from her hair and shoulders. "Get up, girls." Elizabeth helped

Heather to her feet. Lily's eyes filled with tears as Rose helped her up, but she kept quiet. Camellia and Iris rose.

Elizabeth searched the wreckage only to see the body of the driver hunched over what remained of the seat. The horse had broken free and was nowhere in sight. "Come, we must hurry," she said, turning back to the others.

"You're not going anywhere." Horatio was suddenly before them, his short cape billowing in the breeze. He grasped the rope that bound them together and jerked hard, propelling the six of them forward.

Heather fell to her knees at the unexpected motion. "I want to go home."

"Leave us alone," Lily's tiny voice echoed in the morning air, followed by soft sobs.

Iris, who'd been valiantly silent so far, burst into tears until a cacophony of sobs filled the air.

A thunderous look darkened Horatio's face. "Silence. Keep moving!"

Rose paled and bent down beside Heather. She stroked her sister's back. "Shh," she admonished. "We must do what our uncle says."

"Nay." The word erupted from Elizabeth's throat as a fresh surge of anger tore through her. "We will not keep going. In fact, girls, sit down." She set Lily on the ground, then sat beside her.

Rose, Iris, and Camellia joined Heather, Lily, and herself on the ground. The girls' faces were pale and fear glittered in their eyes, but Elizabeth clung to her decision. He couldn't make them all move without someone to help him.

"Get up!" Horatio lurched toward them, his unarmed hand poised to strike.

Elizabeth shifted forward to take the blow, sparing the other girls their uncle's anger.

At Lily's terrified scream, the man's hand jerked to a stop inches from Elizabeth's face.

She remained still. "Let the girls go. I shall go with you."

He grabbed a fistful of her hair and dragged her to her feet. "All of you will get up and keep moving."

"You are going about this all wrong." Elizabeth met his gaze. "The new earl doesn't care about us. He'll be overjoyed to have the estate all to himself now that we are gone."

Horatio's grin became a dark, evil slash. "Nay, he'll come after you, and I'll force him to renounce the title and lands."

Elizabeth forced a smile, praying the girls would remain silent and let her lies erode the man's confidence. "It won't work. He'll never renounce the title. He'll never go back to the Templars. You're a fool to think he would."

"Then I'll kill you all to get what I want." Horatio's hand connected with Elizabeth's cheek. Gasps and cries of distress erupted from the girls as pain exploded on the side of Elizabeth's head. A wave of darkness hovered.

She drew a sharp breath and forced the darkness away. Fainting would help no one. She straightened. "Beating me will not change the situation. You'll never become the Earl of Carrick."

"We'll see about that." He limped away, heading toward the water's edge.

"Our brother does care about us, right?" Lily asked on a new wave of tears.

"Aye, he loves you," Elizabeth whispered near her ear. "I need to trick your uncle."

Lily's mouth formed a silent expression of surprise.

Suddenly the sound of men shouting filled the air. Lucius!

"Has our brother found us?" Camellia whispered.

The echo of hoofbeats sounded in the distance, mingling with the sound of the men's voices. "Aye," Elizabeth said, with a burst of fresh hope. She brought her hands up to her bodice and withdrew a small dirk from between her breasts. At Iris's gasp, Elizabeth brought her fingers to her lips, signaling silence.

Iris pressed her lips together.

"We need to keep stalling and give Lucius a chance to get to us."

Rose gasped, her gaze fixed on where her uncle stood at the bank of the loch. "That might be impossible."

Elizabeth followed her gaze. Limping, Horatio rolled the cask from where it had fallen from the wagon toward the water's edge. He retrieved his sword from where it had fallen and brought the blade down against the side of the cask over and over until a thick black liquid seeped out of the cask and across the surface of the loch. Removing his cape, Horatio dipped the fabric into the liquid then spread the thick tar on the nearby shrubs.

"What's he doing?" Camellia whispered as an acrid scent suddenly filled the air.

Horatio turned to the girls. He smiled crookedly as he

drew a hunk of flint from the folds of his cloak and ran it across the edge of his sword. A spark flared. He struck the sword again and again, sending a flurry of sparks onto the loch. Suddenly, the sparks ignited the thick liquid with a whoosh of sound.

"Let us see if your theory is correct, Miss Huntingdon. Will my nephew come to rescue you girls or let you all burn to death?" Horatio said coldly. "My guess is, he'll try to rescue you. And when he does, I'll be waiting to stab him in the back."

Elizabeth palmed the dirk and worked it over her bonds. She had to set them all free before Horatio could execute his plan. Ruthlessly, she sawed at the rope. Beneath her assault, the twisted coils began severing one by one. Once she was free, she could stay and fight Horatio while the girls escaped.

A louder whoosh startled Elizabeth as red-gold flames rippled along the surface of the loch, gathering speed.

Elizabeth desperately sawed her bonds. She was almost there. Flames on the shrubs licked closer and closer, spreading quickly until they were surrounded by fire. Horatio turned back to them. He held a length of rope in his hands. His eyes glittered brightly in the glare of the fire as he limped toward them. He would tie them here and leave them to die.

With her heart in her throat, Elizabeth slashed once more against the rope. It severed with a snap. She moved to Rose and sawed at the older girl's bonds, until she too was free. Elizabeth passed the dirk to Rose. "Lead the girls out of here. Go. Now!"

Rose shot to her feet, encouraging the others to do the same. "What about you?"

"Go back toward the manor!" Elizabeth cried.

Rose swooped Lily in her arms and headed up the edge of the loch as Elizabeth had directed. The flames leaped from the water to the shrubs and brush along the water's edge. Elizabeth hesitated for a moment. As she watched in horror, the flames curled from the tar-doused shrubs to the branches of the trees until they formed an arc of flame over her head.

"Get back here!" Horatio threw down the rope and drew his sword. He changed direction to follow the girls.

"Nay." The muscles of Elizabeth's stomach knotted with panic. She surged forward. "Run, Rose, run!"

The smoke was thicker now. Elizabeth's eyes stung. Tears streamed down her cheeks. Regardless, she kept her gaze trained on Horatio, preparing for his next move.

He stopped and swung his sword.

Elizabeth stumbled backward as the blade whispered in front of her, nearly missing her middle. She searched the area around her for something with which to defend herself. A cry of despair escaped her when she found no sticks or rocks nearby. The branches overhead crackled and popped with the intensity of the flames.

The smoke grew thicker, blacker, making it harder to see anything. Perhaps that would help the girls escape. The dark figure before her turned back in the direction the girls had disappeared, and Elizabeth blindly leaped forward into Horatio's body. They crashed against the muddy shoreline of the loch. A few feet away the water glowed bright, and black, curling clouds of smoke coiled into the air.

"Get off me!" Horatio made a sound low in his throat.

Sheer terror rode Elizabeth's nerves as she clung to the man's back. He twisted and rolled with her still attached, until he slammed her against the ground. She gasped at the pain that radiated across her back, stealing her breath. Her grip loosened and Horatio sprang free.

The smoke stung her eyes, seared her lungs. She struggled to sit up, but found she could not.

"With all of you dead, there'll be no one to oppose me."

"How? You've left all of us no way to escape. Even yourself," Elizabeth cried.

The man startled as though he suddenly realized what he'd done, not just to the girls and to Lucius, but also himself.

Horatio gripped the sword that had fallen at his feet and charged, his blade pointed at her.

Panic screamed through Elizabeth. She drew a sharp breath. She brought her feet up. As the man lurched forward, intending to skewer her, she kicked out. Her feet connected with his gut.

He lurched sideways into the water. He fell below the surface; then as he came up, an agonized scream filled the air. "I can't swim!" He flailed against the water as flames rippled across his skin and hair.

The stench of burning flesh overwhelmed her senses. Elizabeth pressed a hand to her nose and mouth and clamped her eyes shut. She scooted on her back away from the water's edge. Over Horatio's cries of pain, she could hear men shouting, horses neighing, from somewhere on the opposite shore. For a heartbeat, she felt a pure white-hot flash of hope until the whoosh of the flames shot up next to her, behind her.

Elizabeth stood. Her legs wobbled. She nearly tumbled to the ground once more, but she forced herself to stay upright, to take a step away from the flames.

Fire was all around her, devouring the trees and shrubs like a hungry monster. Curls of black smoke encircled her, searing her lungs and stinging her eyes. Then, above the roar of the flames, Elizabeth heard the sound of splashing water.

She tensed, afraid it was Horatio come back to claim her, until she heard a familiar voice.

"Elizabeth!"

She staggered toward the sound. "Lucius!"

A dark figure surged through the smoke and grabbed her.

"The girls?" she asked.

Lucius's eyes were bright in his soot-stained face. "We found them."

Relief washed through Elizabeth with such force that her knees buckled. Lucius caught her in his arms. "Hold on to me," he said gently.

She clung desperately to Lucius as he half dragged, half carried her through the water.

"Take a deep breath and hold it." Lucius's hand tightened on hers.

The acrid breath she drew hurt her lungs, but she had no time to think of the pain. Heat pressed in around them. She closed her eyes as tears streamed down her cheeks from her stinging eyes.

She couldn't hold her breath any longer. It whooshed out in a painful rush and she was forced to inhale. She was immediately punished by a fit of coughing. She couldn't catch her breath. Panic rushed through her as she began to gasp.

Lucius was coughing too. Dear God, they were going to die in this blackness just as Horatio had planned.

"Elizabeth?" It was Rose's voice.

Elizabeth opened her eyes to see nothing, but she could hear Rose's voice ahead. Was she caught in this hideous trap as well? Hadn't the girls made it to safety?

Elizabeth tried to tell Rose to keep going, but instead of words only gasps pulled from her throat.

"It's all right," Lucius gasped. "We're through."

In that moment, she could see the muted blue-gray sky on the other side of the loch. "Thank...God," she wheezed.

Lucius dragged them ashore and doubled over, still coughing.

"Where are the girls?" Elizabeth asked, searching the lighter gray smoke that hung in the air. "I must see for myself that they are safe."

"I left them here with Lachlan."

At the same moment the smoke around them eased, the sound of the girls' voices came to her. Elizabeth turned. The girls threw themselves into her outstretched arms, weeping and chattering and praising Elizabeth for the fact they were still alive. Elizabeth stroked one blonde head after another and closed her eyes, gathering each girl as close as possible. "It's over," she promised them. "Your uncle is dead."

"Are you certain?" Lucius asked, his voice still roughened by smoke.

Elizabeth set the girls away from her, then stood. "Aye. He fell into his own trap and caught fire. His body, what's left of it, is in the loch." She shuddered.

A moment later she was in Lucius's arms. He gathered her close enough so that she could feel her heart beating against his own.

He stroked the side of her face with his hand. "Are you unharmed?"

She nodded and brushed her cheek against his palm, reassured by his words. "I was so frightened." Once again she paused. "I feared you wouldn't come for me."

"Wouldn't come?" He tipped her face to his. "I'll never leave you." His head dipped down and he pressed his lips to hers.

The girls began to laugh and tease, but Lucius wasn't deterred. He deepened the kiss until Elizabeth was breathless for reasons having nothing to do with the smoke and everything to do with the man who held her in his arms. And yet he still did not say the words she longed to hear. She forced the thought from her head. He would say the words when he was ready.

And if he doesn't?

She stepped out of the circle of his arms. "This is not the time or place."

He nodded and she was thrilled to see a hint of regret pass across his features before he turned away. "We must bury the dead as well—both our own men and the English who were left behind on Scottish soil. Elizabeth, will you take the girls back to the manor?"

"I'll see to them," she said. With a final nod he turned away. Beside her, Lily tugged on Elizabeth's shredded and burnt gown. "Lucius won't leave us, will he?"

"Not like Papa or Marcus?" Iris asked, coming to join Lily at Elizabeth's side.

"Nay," Elizabeth said as she encouraged them forward, toward the manor in the distance. "Not like them."

As she and the girls walked back along the loch, the fire, now out of fuel, died down to a smolder. Elizabeth looked over her shoulder at Lucius. She expected to see sadness reflected in his eyes, but instead of pain, she saw renewal.

The smoke faded. The warmth of the afternoon sun chased the chill away. Elizabeth turned around, hiding the smile upon her lips, and raced for the manor. For the first time since she'd arrived, Elizabeth felt a glimmer of hope that she might find a home with Lucius and his sisters at Midwick Manor.

Chapter Eleven

It was late evening by the time the men had finished the burials. Lucius drifted toward the manor house along with the men. The mood in the air was sober. It had been a long, exhausting day. They'd buried nine men, including what was left of his uncle.

The MacKinleys and the Insleys had been a welcome blessing—as had the other MacKinley clansmen who'd come to help once word reached them about the conflict. Without them, the outcome might have been very different this day.

Lucius looked around him. He could tell by the looks on the men's faces they wanted nothing more than a warm hearth, a hearty meal, a mug of ale, and a good night's sleep as their reward. Yet as the men approached the manor, their tired mumbles became excited chatter at the sight that greeted them there.

Elizabeth and his sisters waited outside, dressed in brightly colored gowns, with greens woven in their hair. They looked fresh and alive and out of place against the graying sky. They greeted the men as they approached and directed them toward several large tubs of warmed water that had been set out for them to wash up.

Before Lucius could get anywhere near Elizabeth, she and the girls slipped inside the manor. Though a sense of disappointment rippled through Lucius at her absence, he had to admit that the water combined with the cool night air renewed his spirit.

Once they were finished, the men were invited into the hall, where they were greeted by the MacKinley clanswomen. While they waited for the men to join them, they'd prepared a feast of boar's head, mincemeat pies, salmon, herring, rabbit stew, roasted onions, bread and cheese, and ale, with frumenty for dessert. Tallow candles set in pairs about the chamber gave the hall a warm and magical air.

It was magical, as everyone was there: Lucius's servants, his crofters, Father Gillian, the Insley and the MacKinley women, Jayne and her children and the midwife, along with his sisters and Elizabeth. The men rushed into the chamber, greeting the others with good cheer and laughter.

A warm smile came to Lucius's lips. He'd had many Christmas Eve feasts in this hall, but none had ever affected him as this one did. Elizabeth had truly taken Midwick Manor and turned it into a place where those who entered felt welcome and loved.

He caught sight of Elizabeth across the chamber and moved toward her. She stopped talking to Silas MacKinley to watch his approach. Her face lit up as he drew near.

Lucius felt himself changing with each step he took across that hall. The shadows of pain and death fell away, and sunlight, pure and hot and white, flooded his body, lighting places that had been cold and dark for years. For the first time in his life he knew what he wanted, and more importantly, he felt as though he deserved it.

When he reached her, he took her hands in his and the rest of the room seemed to fade away, until there were only the two of them. "Elizabeth."

"Welcome home, Lucius."

He was home, and in a place he wanted to share with her for the rest of his days. A thousand things crowded his mind, things he wanted to say, needed to say, until finally the words came to him. "I wasted so many years running away from you, from everyone. I missed so many things, and I wish desperately I could have that time back. But I know that's not possible. So I want the next best thing."

"What's that?" she asked with a hint of worry in her wide brown eyes.

He smiled, wanting her to see what was in his heart. "To make every moment count." His gaze held hers. "I love you, Elizabeth. Will you give me a second chance?"

The words she'd longed to hear sank deep, warmed her heart, and brought tears to her eyes. "Aye, Lucius, I'd give you a million chances if you asked for them." They'd be a family—herself, Lucius, and the girls, along with the children they'd share together someday. She would have a place that was safe with a man who was no fool, who wouldn't gamble their lives or security away.

And suddenly it was too much to bear in silence. Her heart was too full. "I love you, Lucius. I always have."

He kissed her with a passion that made her tremble with need. When he finally released her, the world spun. But he held her close, as though refusing to let go of what they'd just realized they both needed more than food or water or air.

They needed each other.

"I shall never take your love for granted again, my sweet," he whispered against her ear. He pulled away from her then and dropped to his knee. "I know this is a little late, but I must ask you this question and you must promise to answer me truthfully."

"Very well." Her words felt thick in her throat as tears pooled in her eyes once more.

"Miss Elizabeth Huntingdon, will you marry me? Not because you have to, but because you want to?"

He looked at her with a seriousness that made her heart achingly full. "Aye, Lucius, I'll marry you this night. I won't wait another moment to be yours."

Suddenly the room swelled with applause and whoops of cheer. Elizabeth smiled up at her soon-to-be husband, who sealed their promise with a kiss. Laughter rose inside Elizabeth and spilled out in a light, airy sound of pure joy.

"To the altar then?" Lucius asked.

"Aye, please, my love, with all due haste."

Discover Other Books by Gerri Russell

The Stones of Destiny Series

> *THE WARRIOR TRAINER*
> *WARRIOR'S BRIDE*
> *WARRIOR'S LADY*

Other books in Brotherhood of the Scottish Templars Series

> *TO TEMPT A KNIGHT*
> *SEDUCING THE KNIGHT*
> *A KNIGHT TO DESIRE*

Connect with me online:
Twitter: twitter.com/[GerriRussell]
Facebook: facebook.com/[GerriRussell]
Smashwords: smashwords.com/profile/view/ggrussell
Website: GerriRussell.net

Gerri Russell has done it all when it comes to writing; she's worked as a broadcast journalist, newspaper reporter, magazine columnist, technical writer and editor, instructional designer, which all finally led her to follow her heart's desire of being a romance novelist. Gerri is the award-winning author of six novels and one novella. She is best known for her adventurous and emotionally intense novels set in 13th and 14th Century Scottish Highlands. Her most notable series to date is that of the Brotherhood of the Scottish Templars. In her spare time, Gerri is a living history re-enactor with the Shrewsbury Renaissance Faire. A two-time recipient of the Romance Writers of America's Golden Heart award and winner of the American Title II competition sponsored by Dorchester Publishing and RT BOOKreviews Magazine, she lives in Bellevue, Washington with her husband and children.